Whispers of Goodbye

SUE MILLS

Choose the Front Row Media

Published by Choose The Front Row Media

Contact: choosethefrontrow@gmail.com

Cover design by Emily Hensley at smallfrymarketing.com

Editing and Proofreading by Red Adept Editing Services

ISBN Paperback: 979-8-9918300-6-5

Blurbs

Contents

Chapter One

Summer's End

Ten Years Ago

Sam

SAM CARPENTER WINCED AS the morning sun pierced the orange fabric of his two-person tent. *No, it's too early to wake up.* He rolled to his left and gazed at his girlfriend, Quinn Michaels, who was sleeping soundly. His phone buzzed with a message from his brother Matt, telling him their father was in the middle of one of his black moods.

In other words, Matt's telling me to stay away.

Sam noticed the date on his phone. *Two years ago today, Quinn and I went on our first date.* This was Sam's fourth trip to Maine with Quinn, and it was almost over.

Sam eased out of his sleeping bag, pulled on a pair of shorts, and grabbed a shirt before crawling out of the tent. The sun shone brightly, but the air held the morning chill that always set in around the end of August in New England. He retrieved a flannel shirt from his car along with two travel mugs. Stillness washed over him as he made his way along the wooded path to the camp store where coffee waited.

As he left the store carrying coffee and donuts, Mrs. Brossard greeted him. "*Bonjour*, Sam! Stop a minute. I've got bacon." She grinned as Sam changed direction and headed her way.

"You know I can't resist your bacon," he said.

"You go home today?" Mrs. Brossard lived in Quebec and often apologized for her broken English. Sam always told her it was better than his French. The kindly grandmother and her husband spent the entire summer at the campground, often entertaining their grandchildren.

"Yup, home today, and Quinn leaves for college on Wednesday." He munched on a strip of bacon. "I don't know how you do it. Your bacon is the best."

"You're going to miss your pretty lady, but you'll be fine. Time will go fast. Next thing you know, it will be summer again, and we'll be back here."

"And you'll be chasing after those grandkids and cooking me bacon." He gathered Mrs. Brossard into a hug. "Have a wonderful winter."

"You, too, Sam. Tell Quinn to stop and say goodbye before you leave."

Sam followed a path to the edge of a cliff overlooking the Atlantic Ocean. The trail marked the boundary of the campground, and Sam walked toward a small trailer parked in a clearing surrounded by towering pine trees.

"Bonjour, Sam." Philippe Desjardins waved a hand, inviting Sam into the campsite. "I'm burning the last of our wood supply before we leave. Sylvie is at the bathhouse, making herself beautiful. Or, should I say, more beautiful?"

Sam and Quinn had met Philippe and his girlfriend Sylvie in July. They were a year older than Sam and lived in Quebec City.

Sam offered Philippe a donut. "This is the best spot in the campground. I'm glad you had it so Quinn and I could visit."

"I think they put us here so if we indulged in any bad habits"—Philippe wiggled his eyebrows suggestively—"no one can hear or see us. You know I'm right."

Sam laughed. "Not that you or Sylvie would ever do that."

Quinn

Quinn Michaels splashed cold water on her face, hoping to calm the puffy redness of her eyes.

"Don't move." Her friend Sylvie dug into her makeup bag and came out with concealer. "Turn toward me."

As Sylvie applied the concealer, Quinn said, "I'm such a mess. I try not to cry in front of Sam, but he was gone when I woke up this morning, and all I could think of was how in a few days, I'll be alone every morning, ten hours away from home." She closed her eyes, and Sylvie continued to work on her face.

"He'll never know." After a second, Sylvie stepped back. "Voilà. You look beautiful again. Come to our campsite. I bet Sam is there. We're burning the last of our firewood."

As they walked along the wooded path, Quinn asked, "Are you sad about leaving?"

"So very sad. Going back to school in Ithaca will be difficult." Sylvie sighed and shook her head. "This summer has been magical." Philippe and Sylvie had worked as recreation directors at a nearby summer camp while living in the camper. "It's been our first chance to live together outside of our parents' houses. And once this last year of university is done, we'll be together all the time!"

"Are you talking about marriage?"

Sylvie laughed. "*Mais bien sur!* Of course! I'm a traditional girl. I want a proposal. We'll invite you and Sam to the wedding." The campsite came into view, as did the two men. Sylvie kissed Philippe before sitting beside him.

Sam stood and wrapped Quinn in his arms. "I'm glad you're here." He handed her a donut and the coffee mug before offering the donuts to Sylvie.

Sylvie leaned against Philippe. "Quinn and I were talking about the big separation about to happen, with me heading to Ithaca and her to Virginia."

"I don't want to think about it." Quinn took a swallow of her coffee despite her churning stomach. "I don't know why I thought going to school so far away from home was a good idea." She looked at Sam. "Say the word, and I'll change my plans."

"Oh no. I'm not doing that and having you resent me ten years from now." Sam frowned and shook his head, then he gave Quinn a sad smile. "Even though you being so far away is going to kill me."

Philippe waved his hand. "Just a little farther than my Sylvie is from me. Look at us—we've survived it. Only one quick school year left." He stood and reached out to Sylvie to pull her up and into his arms.

"We're going to stop at Old Orchard Beach before we head to Vermont," Quinn said. She looked at Sam, who nodded in agreement. "Can you come with us?"

Philippe and Sylvie both nodded. The fire was already dying down, and Philippe threw some dirt on it. They all agreed to meet at the beach in an hour.

As they walked back to their campsite, Quinn held Sam's hand. "I'm so glad we met them. Sylvie told me they'd invite us to their wedding."

Sam pulled her close. "That would be fun. I've never been to Quebec City."

Most of their gear was packed, and after they stuffed the tent into a duffel, they hopped into Sam's battered car. Before they drove out of the campground, Sam stopped at the store so Quinn could jump out.

She ran over to Mrs. Brossard's campsite and smiled at the kindly woman. "I couldn't leave without saying goodbye."

Mrs. Brossard wrapped her arms around Quinn. "I will miss you, *ma petite*, but we'll see you next summer. Then you can show off all that you've learned!"

Quinn fought back tears. "I'll do that. Give Mr. Brossard a hug for me, and I hope you have a great winter." With that, Quinn climbed back into Sam's car. She rolled down the window and waved as they drove away, calling, *"Au revoir!"*

Sam reached for Quinn's hand, bringing it to his mouth for a kiss. "They're good people."

"Yes." Quinn squeezed his hand. "Mrs. Brossard's like the grandmother I never had."

Crowds of people enjoying the last warm days of the Maine summer covered the long stretch of sand at Old Orchard Beach, but Quinn and Sam found their favorite spot unoccupied. They spread out a blanket and towels, and a few minutes later, Philippe and Sylvie arrived.

"One last game of volleyball?" Sylvie suggested with a smile on her face.

Quinn smirked. "You mean one last time for you to trounce us."

The four of them ambled over to the waiting net and played a spirited game until a spike from Philippe sent Sam diving, only to miss the ball and fall to the sand. Quinn leapt to prevent it from landing, but the ball skittered away from her. She fell on top of Sam, and Philippe collapsed in laughter as Sylvie declared victory.

Quinn got to her feet. "No more volleyball. It's too hot, and your height must be giving you an advantage because you beat us every time." She grabbed Sam's hand, pulling him up. "Race you to the water!"

The four of them ran over the sand until they reached the water's edge. Quinn and Sylvie both plunged into the chilly waves, surfacing ten feet from shore.

"Come on, chickens!" Quinn called. "Get yourselves out here!"

Sam couldn't match Quinn in swimming, and Philippe didn't like the cold, so both men took their time entering the water. They walked in until the waves lapped their knees.

"Oh, *c'est froid*," Philippe growled. "So cold!"

The men stood like statues, letting the surf wash over them, while the girls smirked. Finally, a swell crashed against them, and both men screamed as the cold water hit their manhood. Philippe dove under the waves, coming up beside Sylvie. Sam was close behind him, surfacing in front of Quinn.

"You squealed like little girls," Quinn teased.

"I'm shriveled like a raisin," Sam said. "I'll never recover."

Philippe shook his head. "Sylvie, I'm going to be no use to you."

They all laughed and continued to play in the ocean until Quinn began to shiver. They walked to shore and lay on their towels, letting the scorching sun dry them. Quinn rested her hand on Sam's back and slid her body closer to his. "We can go to Virginia Beach when you come to visit me at school. The water there is warmer than the Maine coast."

"I can't wait. I'm glad your parents are taking me with them for Family Weekend."

"I'll die if you don't come. You're the one I'll want to see." Quinn sat up. "I'm sure I will miss my parents, but nothing like

I'll miss you." She leaned over and kissed him before standing. "I'm hungry. Let's go up on the boardwalk."

Sylvie got to her feet. "We must say goodbye. The camp is having an end of summer party." She hugged Quinn. "Let me know how college is for you. I think you will love it." She bent over to kiss Sam's cheek. "You be a good boy while she is gone."

"Always." He fist-bumped Philippe. "Till next summer."

Quinn could hear the sadness in Sam's words.

Our magical summer is over.

On the boardwalk, Quinn pulled Sam into a photo booth and fed money into it. They smiled widely for the first picture, kissed for the second, and stuck their tongues out at the camera in the third. For the final picture, Sam wrapped his fingers in Quinn's hair, kissing her passionately.

They looked at the photos later as they walked along the boardwalk. Quinn's dark hair contrasted with Sam's light brown, which had bleached out to nearly blond from working outside all summer. His icy-blue eyes sparkled against his sun-kissed face. Quinn sighed. *I love him so much.*

She tore the strip in half, handing him the bottom two. "This will be the first thing I put on my bulletin board," she told him.

They ordered lobster rolls and sat at the end of the board-walk to eat and enjoy the late-afternoon sun. Sam finished his and looked at Quinn. "Are you going to find these in Virginia?"

She laughed. "Probably not, and if I do, they won't be as good. But I think there will be crab cakes, and those are pretty tasty."

After Sam returned from taking care of the trash, he said, "Let's take one last walk on the beach."

He held Quinn's hand as they walked with their heads down, looking for shells. Suddenly, he dropped her hand and took a few steps toward the water. He bent down, snatched something off the sand, and returned to Quinn with a triumphant grin on his face. "A sand dollar!"

Quinn beamed at him. "That is cool! Let me look closer. I've never seen one outside of gift shops."

He handed it to her. "You keep it. A reminder of the summer."

"It's been perfect. I'll remember it forever." She kissed him and kept the sand dollar on her lap throughout the drive to Vermont.

Chapter Two

<h1 style="text-align: center;">The Departure</h1>

Sam

SAM WAS STRUGGLING TO keep himself together in the face of Quinn's tears. "Quinn, babe, you need to stop."

It was after seven in the morning on departure day for Quinn, but she had cried in Sam's arms all night long. Quinn's mother had knocked on the door twice, saying they needed to get on the road. The drive to Virginia would be long, and he knew her parents wanted to leave early. That plan was drifting away as Quinn could not stop crying and would not leave his arms.

Sam was worn out. Exhaustion filled every muscle after helping pack the car for the trip to Virginia and getting no sleep. He heard the heavy footsteps of Mr. Michaels in the hall. "Quinn Michaels. I know this is difficult, but you must get up and into the car. We should already be on our way." His tone left no room for discussion.

Quinn disentangled herself from Sam and walked to the bathroom.

Sam found Quinn's parents in the kitchen. "She didn't sleep at all," he said. He poured a cup of coffee and joined them at the table. "I'm surprised at what a difficult time she's having. She told me from the very beginning about her plans to get out of this town after high school."

Mrs. Michaels laughed. "Quinn's been telling us that since she was ten years old. We appreciate you not pressuring her to change her mind. She needs this." She put her coffee cup down and wiped away a tear. "We're going to miss her too."

The Michaelses had become like family to him, allowing him to stay in their house on the weekends when he returned to his hometown from college. They'd welcomed him into a warm family atmosphere, one free from the angry, alcohol-fueled outbursts that he'd grown up with.

And with Quinn at college ten hours away, I'll have to stay at my house all the time. I'm going to miss them.

A few minutes later, Sam gave Quinn one last embrace before she huddled into the tiny space left in the car's back seat.

Mr. Michaels clapped Sam on the shoulder. "We'll see you in a few days. Thanks for looking after things here while we're gone." They'd planned to make a couple of stops on their drive home, so Sam would stay at their house until they returned.

Sam stood, watching forlornly, as the car drove away then stumbled back to Quinn's bed. He stripped down to his boxers and pulled the covers over his head. Her scent lingered, and he breathed deeply, already missing the feel of her in his arms. He fell asleep and slept for several hours.

A text from Quinn was waiting when Sam awoke, letting him know they were halfway to the campus. Sam got up, did his laundry, and planned out what he needed for the upcoming semester. He would be interning with a local architecture firm and living at home. Being around his father would be miserable, but it would save money.

Early in the evening, his phone pinged with a text from his brother.

> *Matt: I know Quinn left today. Why don't you come to the Whistle Stop for a drink or two?*

Sam thought about it. Matt had graduated along with Quinn from high school in June, but he had no interest in college. Instead, he'd been working at the same factory as their father since graduation. Matt was only eighteen, but Sam knew he used a fake ID to buy alcohol.

I'll go to make sure he stays out of trouble.

Once he arrived at the Whistle Stop, Sam went up to the bar for a soda before fighting his way through the crowd to find his brother, pausing along the way to bump fists with guys he remembered from high school.

Eventually, he located Matt, who greeted him loudly. "There you are! How did the goodbyes go?"

Sam pulled out a chair and settled at the table, joining Matt and his friends. "It was brutal. But I talked to Quinn a little bit ago, and she sounded better. They're at a hotel. She'll move into her room tomorrow."

Sam hadn't been to the Whistle Stop before, so he looked around, getting his bearings. There were three pool tables in the back near the bar and a dance floor at the front of the building. He noticed secluded nooks with tables for two. *I wish I was sitting at one of those tables with Quinn right now.*

Matt grabbed Sam's glass, took a swallow, and shook his head. "What the hell is this? You will not turn into an alcoholic from one drink!"

Sam snatched his glass back. "What I drink is none of your business."

The music started up, and everyone at the table but Sam made their way to the dance floor. A pretty blond girl with blue eyes walked up to him and grabbed his hand, trying to tug him out of his chair.

Sam shook his head. He leaned toward her so she could hear him and said, "Sorry, I don't dance."

The girl sat down beside him. "I'm Ginger. I've never seen you here before." She wore a denim skirt and a red tank top. She leaned in, making no effort to conceal her cleavage.

Sam shoved his chair back to put some distance between them. "It's my first time."

"Where have you been hiding?"

"I go to college in Maine, but I'm home this semester, doing an internship in St. Johnsbury." He thought for a minute. "My girlfriend isn't old enough to drink, so this hasn't been a hang-out for us."

"But you're here tonight."

"She left for college today. My brother Matt invited me to join him."

Her blue eyes lit up. "Matt Carpenter?"

Sam nodded.

"My friend Jilly likes him, but he doesn't seem interested. I know Matt has two brothers. Are you Sam or Joe?"

"Sam."

Ginger continued to sit at the table, making conversation with Sam until he left. Matt could apparently take care of himself, and Sam wasn't interested in dancing or drinking—he just missed Quinn.

Quinn

Quinn trudged across campus after lunch. Ten days had passed since Sam hugged her goodbye in the driveway, and she was miserable and lonely.

I might as well be starting high school instead of college. I'm afraid to speak to new people, and no one has made any effort to reach out to me.

Her roommate, Wendy, was friendly but totally absorbed with her boyfriend, who lived on the floor below them. He visited their room frequently, making Quinn jealous of the time they spent together. Watching them made her ache for Sam.

From the day she chose this college, Quinn had known the bulk of the students came from within a two-hour drive of the campus, but she hadn't realized that most would leave every weekend. It was her second Saturday there, and she felt like she was walking through a ghost town, half expecting a tumbleweed to careen by. She'd eaten lunch at a table by herself, and she would spend Saturday afternoon studying.

At least her classes were the one area that had not disappointed her. She liked all of her professors, and the coursework was challenging but not overwhelming. Losing herself in homework eased the pain of missing Sam.

At four in the afternoon, Quinn slammed her anatomy book closed and jumped off her bed. Pictures of Sam dominated her side of the room. She trailed her fingers over the poster she'd made with photos taken during the summer. She smiled at one of her with Sylvie and at one of Sylvie with Philippe. Her fingers lingered on the two photos of her and Sam in the photo booth. *Oh, how I wish I were kissing him right now.*

She climbed back onto her bed and wrapped a cheetah-print blanket over her shoulders, then she picked up the phone to call Sam, taking deep breaths while she waited to hear his voice.

He answered on the first ring. "Hey, babe. How are you?"

I will not cry. I will not cry. "I'm okay, just finished my anatomy homework. What are you doing?"

Sam launched into a long description of how he and Matt had spent the day cutting down trees at their father, Trent's, command. Quinn lost herself in the sound of his voice and imagined being in Vermont, watching him work in the woods.

After Sam finished talking about Trent's project, he asked, "Will you do something tonight? Go to the movies? Don't they screen films every Saturday?"

I will not cry. I will not cry. "I think I've seen the movie that's showing." She had been hiding her sadness from Sam. Texting made it easier, since she could cry as she typed "I miss you," and he would never know. Her week had been busy enough that when he'd last called her, just before she went to sleep the night before, she'd been able to fool him into thinking she was fine. *I don't know if I can do that today.* "How about you? What are your plans tonight?"

"I went to the Whistle Stop with Matt last night. I might go again tonight."

He's going on about his life without me. "Is Matt old enough to go there?" *I will not cry. I will not cry.*

Sam laughed. "No. He has a fake ID. But the bar doesn't pay attention. Julie and Casey were there. I sat with them."

Quinn pictured her best friend, Julie, and her boyfriend sitting with Sam, enjoying drinks and dancing or playing pool. "D-did you dance?" Her resolve broke.

Sam scoffed. "The only girl I want to dance with is at college in Virginia. I miss you so much."

"I miss you too." Her sniffing increased, and she knew Sam could hear it.

"Babe, are you crying?"

"Y-y-yes." Her voice became unsteady.

"Babe, what's wrong? I know we're missing each other, but I thought everything was okay. Your classes, your roommate..."

By then, Quinn was full-on sobbing, much like the morning she'd left. Through her tears, she described her unhappiness.

Sam

Sam's heart broke as he listened to Quinn. She had sounded so good every time they talked before. He'd worried about her moving away from him, not only physically but emotionally as well. These tears painted a different picture.

"I'm acting like I did the year you met me, Sam. I sit in the back of the classroom, knowing the answers, but I don't raise my hand. Some professors randomly call on students, and when that happens to me, I can feel my face getting red. Then I stammer through the answer even though I know the material. I can't do this, Sam." Her voice dissolved into sobs.

"Yes, you can, babe. It'll become easier. Remember how hard my first weeks of college were? We'd just started dating, and I missed you. I didn't know anyone—"

"Sam, you've never gone through anything like this. You talk to everyone! I walk between classes all by myself. It's like high school. Everyone already knows someone except for me."

"You'll make friends. Can't Wendy introduce you to people?"

"She's all tied up with her boyfriend. I'm—I'm jealous of them." Her sobbing continued and intensified.

Sam didn't know how to comfort her through the distance between them, but he tried. After they'd talked for almost two hours, Quinn repeated what she had said earlier. "I'm all alone this weekend. I want to come home." She drew an uneven breath. "I can't stay here. I can't do it, Sam."

Sam got up and found his backpack. "Quinn, I'm coming to see you." He began throwing in enough clothes for several days.

"I know. You're coming with my parents in a few weeks. I won't survive that long."

"No, baby. I'm coming tonight. If I leave now, I'll be there by morning. My internship doesn't start for another week, and I have nothing to do except work for my father. I miss you, and you're breaking my heart. I can't stay here while you're so upset."

"You're going to come?"

"I'm getting in the car. Hear the ignition? Keep your bed warm for me, babe."

Chapter Three

The Visit

Quinn

TEN HOURS LATER, SAM arrived at her dorm. He broke into a wide grin at the sight of Quinn sitting on the curb waiting for him. She stood as Sam jumped out of the car, and they met halfway across the parking lot. She launched herself into his arms, wrapping her legs around his waist, both of them laughing and crying.

"I can't believe you're here," Quinn said. "Or that your car made it all the way."

Sam laughed. "I know. God, I've missed you. Can we go to your room?"

Sam passed out almost as soon as his head hit the pillow, and Quinn watched him sleep, feeling happy for the first time since her arrival in Virginia. She curled up against him and slept for a few hours.

When she woke, she texted Wendy, telling her about Sam's visit. She smiled at the reply—Wendy said she would spend the week with her boyfriend, letting Quinn and Sam have the room to themselves.

Quinn watched Sam's eyes flutter open then leaned in to kiss him. "Hey."

He reached out to her. "You're too far away. Come here." Their lips met again when she was in his arms, and Quinn opened her mouth, inviting him in. She relished the thrust of his tongue against hers.

Sam had removed his jeans before he crawled under the covers, and Quinn reached over to stroke his erection through his boxers, her breath coming faster. Sam fondled her breasts, and a sigh escaped him. He reached for the hem of her shirt. "Can I take this off?"

"Please. And then take yours off."

He gently pulled her shirt off, and his eyes grew wide when he saw she wore no bra. His tongue brushed her nipples, which pebbled in response, then he tugged his shirt over his head. "I want to feel you next to me." He hugged her against him. "Are you braless all the time? Is that a thing here?"

"Only for you, babe." Her hand returned to his erection. "You're hard. Someone would think you hadn't gotten laid in a while." She squeezed him gently.

"Someone would be right. That hand doesn't need to stay on the outside."

Quinn smiled as she continued to stroke his cock through the boxers. "Is that mouth going to do anything other than talk?"

Sam lowered his mouth to her breast, circling her nipple with his tongue and then sucking hard. Quinn shuddered in response and slid her hand into his boxers.

They played for a few minutes, thrusting against each other and sighing in pleasure. Sam's fingers delved into Quinn's panties, searching for her slit. Her breath caught when he found it, and she moaned, "We need to get naked." She shimmied out of her underwear, and Sam stood to remove his boxers. "I bought condoms. They're in that drawer." She pointed to the nightstand.

Sam opened the drawer and chuckled. "What are you expecting?"

Quinn knew he was talking about the size of the box. "A very horny boyfriend." She watched him sheathe himself. "Was I wrong?"

"God no." He climbed back on the bed. His mouth went to her breasts, and his hand reached for her core. He thrust one finger, then two, inside. "You're wet."

"Umm." Quinn wrapped her hand around his cock.

"Babe, I'm not going to last."

"I've missed this." Quinn let go of him and pulled him on top of her. "I need you inside. Show me you want me."

He hovered over her for a moment then eased his way in. He remained still for a few seconds. "Can't hold back."

"Don't want you to."

Quinn met his frantic thrusts, orgasming seconds before Sam groaned and collapsed onto her. After a moment, he rolled onto his side, holding Quinn tightly to him. Breathless, he moaned, "Oh, baby, I didn't know how much I was missing you."

At lunch on Tuesday, Sam pushed his tray along the counter in the dining hall. "Have you explored the campus?"

"Not really."

They found a table. Tuesday was Quinn's easy day, and she was excited to spend the afternoon with Sam.

"I walked all over yesterday while you were in class. I'm going to show you around. It's a nice campus." He took a bite of his hamburger. "The food's good. Better than Winthrop."

"I didn't think the food in your dining hall was bad when I visited you. Are you missing being on campus there?"

"I'm not wild about being at my parents' house, but I'm excited about my internship."

"Have you seen my parents?"

"Not since the day they got home after bringing you here. I feel weird seeing them without you."

"They ask about you every time I talk to them. They think of you like a son—you know that." Quinn took a bite of her sandwich. "You should visit them."

Sam nodded. After they finished eating, he took her hand and led her outside. They climbed the hill to reach the athletic complex and went inside the field house. "This is an awesome pool. You need to keep swimming. You know that relieves your stress."

"I know." Quinn looked at the floor. "I feel awkward coming by myself."

Sam put his arms around her. "It'll only be uncomfortable the first couple of times." He rubbed circles on her back before letting her go.

That afternoon, they traversed every inch of the campus. At one point, they turned onto a secluded path. A chipmunk ventured out from the trees, and Quinn snapped her arm out. "Stop!" She took a step, hoping to get closer to it, but it scampered into the woods. "That was cute."

The path ended at a riverbank. Quinn sank onto the bench at the edge of the river, and Sam sat down beside her. She laid her head on his shoulder. "This is nice," she said. "I know what you're doing."

"What am I doing?"

"You're making me see all the good things. Telling me the food is delicious. Suggesting that I go swimming." She took his hand. "You're showing me how to be happy."

Sam gave her fingers a squeeze. "Is it working?"

"Maybe. I acted like a baby on the phone. I'm sorry you felt like you needed to drive down here and rescue me." Then she grinned at him. "But I'm not sorry that you're here."

"I'm glad I came. It's going to be easier for me, being able to picture you." He lowered his lips to hers.

After several minutes of kissing, Quinn pulled away. "Tell me about the Whistle Stop."

"What's to tell? It's a bar."

"I want to picture you."

Sam smiled. "Okay, that's fair. The owner is loose about IDs. Matt and his friends all have fake ones so they can drink. There's a dance floor, and Thursday through Saturday, there's a DJ. There are three pool tables. I spend quite a bit of time playing pool."

"Do kids who graduated with me hang out there?"

"Yeah. Julie and Casey, Tiff, Chuck and Davey, and some guys from my class."

"Do you drink?"

"I get one beer and make it last until I leave. I'd wondered how much Matt drank, but he doesn't seem to have more than a couple."

"Because of your dad."

"Bingo. There's also a girl named Jilly who hangs around with us. She's got it bad for Matt, but he's ignoring her."

On Thursday, they went back to the bench by the river. It had rained all day on Wednesday, and the river threatened to overflow its banks. The roar of the water over the rocks made conversation difficult, so instead, Sam kept his lips locked on Quinn's. His hands slid under her T-shirt, and he shifted his hips in his pants, trying to make room for his growing erection.

Quinn pulled back from him. "What's wrong? You're into me, but I can tell something is bothering you."

Sam stood and grabbed Quinn's hand. They walked upstream to a quieter spot. "My mom called. My dad's pissed that I'm gone. He expected me to work for him all week. They bought a new property that needs rehabbing. Not sure what I'll be facing when I go home."

"Should you leave now? I'm okay. Really."

He bent down and picked up a rock, turning it in his fingers, then flung it into the water. "Nope. I'm staying until Saturday. A couple more days won't make a difference."

Quinn wrapped her arms around him. "I'm sorry he's so hard on you."

"Yeah, me too." He sighed and hugged her tighter.

On Friday night, they climbed the stairs to the bell tower to watch the sunset. They stood wrapped in each other's arms, watching the sky turn vivid shades of pink and red.

Quinn sighed. "I'll be okay now. Being able to remember you here will make it easier. Thank you for coming. It means everything to me." She punctuated her words with a kiss.

The colors faded, and as darkness began to descend, Quinn said, "We should go to my room. One more night before you start the drive to Vermont early tomorrow." She moved toward the stairs.

Sam held tight to her arm. "Wait a minute." He drew her to him. "I love you, and I'd do anything for you. This week has been unforgettable." He caressed her cheek. "I want to marry you."

Quinn nodded.

Sam spoke again, his voice thick with emotion. "I want... When you come home at Christmas, I want us to get engaged. I want my ring on your finger. Do you want that too?"

"I do, Sam—you know I do. We've talked about our future together forever."

His face erupted in a huge smile. "I promise I'll surprise you with a romantic proposal. I can't wait!"

They walked back arm in arm, and in the morning, Quinn let Sam leave with only a few tears.

THE FIRST GOODBYE

Chapter Four

Making Friends

Quinn

THE SAME BOY SAT next to Quinn in Algebra every day, and he was always late, so when he arrived early on the Monday after Sam left, it shocked her. The boy leaned over and asked, "Did you do the homework?"

Well, duh, of course I did the homework. She nodded. "Yes."

"Don't look like that. Not everybody does." He grinned. "I pegged you for someone who always gets it done. What did you get for number sixteen?"

He'd picked the one problem she'd struggled with. "I'm not sure my answer is right. That one took me longer to get than all the rest of them."

"I didn't even get an answer. Can we compare our work?" He pulled his chair closer to Quinn's and laid his paper on the table. They went over the steps, and just as the professor stepped into the classroom, the boy slumped back. "That was my mistake, right there. Your answer is right. Thanks."

After class, the boy said, "I'm Mason, and you're Quinn, right?"

She nodded.

"I remember because it's an unusual name. Gotta get to my next class. See you Wednesday."

Over the next week or two, Mason continued to talk to her before algebra class, then a girl from her anatomy class invited her to a comedy show. Quinn became more comfortable, and when she spoke to Sam from then on, she didn't have to pretend to be happy.

Sam

Sam's internship started, and the respect he received from the experienced architects thrilled him. His relationship with his father remained rocky, with Trent continuing to drink excessively and sinking into dark moods. Sam tried to stay away.

His colleagues at the office often invited him to join them for drinks after work, but he preferred hanging out at the Whistle Stop with Matt. His pool game was improving, and he had developed new friendships. Jilly was a constant fixture at their table, and Matt had finally noticed her interest. Wherever Jilly was, Ginger followed, and Sam watched to see who she got involved with. He would rather have been with Quinn, but the happenings at the Whistle Stop filled the empty spots for him.

Sam had started looking at rings when he returned from his impromptu visit and had finally decided on a style. He ordered it just before he traveled to Virginia with Quinn's parents for Family Weekend. Neither he nor Quinn had told anyone about their agreement to become engaged at Christmas time, and they spent the weekend basking in their secret. She teased him without mercy, trying to find out what ring he'd chosen, but he remained resolute about keeping it a mystery.

Quinn would be home for a visit at Thanksgiving, and the holiday could not come soon enough for Sam.

Quinn

In algebra class the day after Sam and her parents went home, Mason startled Quinn out of her daydreams about Family Weekend. "This is getting more and more difficult for me, but you're breezing through it," he said. "Any chance I could study with you?"

"Um, yeah, I guess so. I study in the library to give my roommate time alone with her boyfriend." *My God, why did I tell him that?*

Mason raised his eyebrows suggestively. "Does she do the same for you?"

"No. I mean—no, I don't need that." *Tell him you have a boyfriend at home.* The professor started his lecture at that moment, and Quinn fretted about the exchange with Mason for the rest of the class.

Before they left the room, Mason asked, "What time should I meet you?"

"Does three on Tuesday and Thursday work for you?"

He nodded and said, "I'll see you then," before he ambled off.

Quinn sent Sam a text telling him about her new study buddy. Sam texted back, asking if he should be jealous, and Quinn assured him he had nothing to worry about.

She walked nervously into the library at three, and Mason arrived shortly afterward.

"I got lost about two weeks ago." He flipped through his book until he found the problems that had given him trouble.

They worked for an hour, reviewing the prior lessons then doing the homework for the next day.

"Are you a freshman?" Mason asked.

When Quinn nodded, he said, "I'm a sophomore. I took a Math for Dummies course last year."

Quinn hid her laughter. "Is that Math 000?"

"Might as well be. I didn't test well, so I couldn't skip the remedial course." He ran his hand through his hair. "I appreciate this. Let's exchange cell numbers in case one of us can't make it. Then neither of us has to wait unnecessarily."

That night, Sam asked her about Mason, and Quinn described how poor his algebra skills were. She didn't tell Sam about the lengthy text conversation she'd had with Mason after he sent her a *GIF* about letters not belonging in math.

Two days later, when Quinn walked into the dining hall, Mason waved her over to his table. "Sit with us." He looked around at his friends. "This is Quinn. She's the one who's going to get me through Algebra."

The table was full, and they all seemed to know each other. Quinn nervously slid into the one empty chair. Mason's friends asked Quinn questions to get acquainted and shared information about themselves. She was the only freshman in the group, and she enjoyed being accepted by older students. One guy told a joke, and Quinn laughed more than she had since she left Vermont.

That night, when Sam called, Quinn had text convos going with Mason and with one of the girls she had met at his table. Those conversations had her distracted, and she struggled to think of anything to say to Sam. They hung up after only five minutes.

What is going on? I've never talked to Sam for such a short time. But it's the same old conversation every night between us.

At lunch on Thursday, Mason's group was talking about a party the next night at one of the fraternities, and they invited Quinn to join them. Quinn hesitated, and Leigh, a girl who lived in Quinn's residence hall, noticed. "We can go together," Leigh said. "I hate walking into parties by myself. Does that bother you too?"

When Quinn nodded, Leigh smiled. "Great! It's a date."

Will Sam mind? He tells me all the time that he wants me to have fun, and he goes out every night.

Via text, Quinn told Sam they had invited her to a party, and he responded enthusiastically. "Call me when you get home, please," he sent. "I enjoy talking to you before I go to bed."

"Of course I will. I feel the same way. I love you."

Leigh knocked at her door while Quinn was getting ready. "What should I wear?" Quinn asked.

"Skinny jeans and a tank top," Leigh said. "It'll look hot. You have a great ass. The jeans will show it off."

As they walked to the frat house, Quinn said, "I don't need to show off my butt. I'm not looking for a guy. I have a boyfriend."

"Here?"

"No, at home."

"And how far away is that?" After Quinn told her, Leigh shook her head. "And you both plan to remain faithful?"

Quinn's steps slowed. "Of course!"

Leigh raised her hands. "Hey, no offense. It's difficult. My boyfriend is at school four hours from here. We started last year thinking we would stay committed, but then we both found ourselves attracted to other people. We took a break until the end of the school year." She paused. "We agreed that we could each do whatever we wanted, no questions asked, and in the spring, we'd see where we were."

"What did you do? How far did you go?"

"Far enough to show me that Billy is the one for me." Leigh must have seen the curiosity in Quinn's eyes, because she went on. "I dated a couple of boys. We took it all the way. I needed to know. The sex was mediocre, but even more important, my feelings for them weren't the same."

Quinn nodded. She believed there was a close connection between making love and being in love. "Maybe the sex wasn't great because of the lack of emotion."

"Maybe," Leigh said, then she snickered. "Although I have friends who tell me about their mind-blowing orgasms with guys who are no more than one-night stands."

"Do you think your boyfriend did the same?"

Leigh shrugged. "I imagine he did. We agreed not to delve into the details. Our relationship is stronger now than it ever was."

Quinn frowned. "I don't think I could do that, and I know Sam wouldn't. He was at college the past two years and wasn't with anyone else."

"You're young. Wouldn't you rather find out now that someone else is better suited to you than after a ten- or fifteen-year marriage?" She turned off the sidewalk onto a walkway to a large house. "This is the place."

Quinn and Leigh walked into the party at nine thirty, and the raucous atmosphere immediately overwhelmed Quinn. Music with pounding bass played, and someone shoved a plastic cup into her hand. Leigh leaned over, shouting to be heard. "It's spiked punch. There's a keg around somewhere too. And we can find a joint, if that's your preference."

A guy Quinn recognized from lunch materialized and put his arms around Leigh, pulling her into a group of people moving to the music.

Before she left her room, Quinn had decided that she would not drink. She'd never drank alcohol before, and the thought of losing control scared her.

Feeling awkward and alone, Quinn watched the hordes of people wandering through the room, desperately searching for someone to talk to. Her gaze shifted to the cup in her hand. *I wonder what it tastes like?* She knew one swallow of alcohol wouldn't make her drunk. *One sip won't hurt.* She took a tentative swallow and choked as the sweet liquid burned its way down her throat. *Oh my God, that's terrible.*

Mason came over and put his arm over her shoulder. "There's my little mathematician. Do you need more to drink?" He peered into her cup. "Nope, looks like you're all set for a few. Great party, huh?" He wandered off before Quinn could reply.

Quinn placed the cup of punch on a table and watched the people around her dancing, making out in the corners, and laughing hysterically. A boy she recognized from anatomy class approached her, cocked his head toward the dancers, and took her hand, pulling her in that direction. Quinn resisted for a moment, then she decided dancing would be better than standing around, especially as the only sober person in the building.

They danced to several songs before the boy drifted off in search of a beer. He returned and started dancing with Quinn again. Midway through that song, he started grinding on her, and Quinn backed away. Dancing was one thing. Having a drunk, sweaty body up against her was something else.

Quinn was ready to leave but felt reluctant to walk across campus by herself, so she waited for Leigh. At close to midnight, Leigh appeared, and she entertained Quinn all the way back to her room with tales of her evening. Exhausted, Quinn fell onto her bed, asleep in seconds.

Chapter Five

Distractions

Sam

WHAT THE HELL WAS she doing?

Sam had waited all night for Quinn's call that didn't come. He awoke early in the morning, amazed that he'd slept at all, and looked at his phone, where the text messages he'd sent Quinn the night before sat unread.

I'm not waiting any longer. He called Quinn and waited impatiently for her to answer.

"Hello?" Quinn sounded confused and sleepy.

"Why didn't you call me?" Sam tried to keep his voice soft, but he knew the aggravation and worry he was feeling crept into it.

"Sam? What time is it? Is something wrong?"

"You were supposed to call me last night."

"Oh God, I'm sorry. I fell asleep as soon as I lay down. It was after midnight."

"I was worried." Sam's tone softened. "Did you have fun?"

Quinn laughed. "It was okay. I'm certain I was the only sober person there. Drunk people are very amusing."

"Yeah, they can be," Sam agreed, relieved to know she hadn't gotten drunk. "You didn't drink anything?"

"One sip of some nasty punch." She shared more details about the party, then added, "I was bored after an hour, but I didn't want to walk across campus alone. When I danced with the guy from my anatomy class..."

"You danced with someone?" Sam hadn't expected that.

"Yeah, he asked me, and I was just standing around." Quinn yawned. "Are you upset?"

"Well, I don't like the idea."

"What are you doing all those nights at the bar?"

"I'm not dancing with anyone! I play pool."

"So sorry, there wasn't a pool table at the house," Quinn snapped back. "I need to pee. Can we talk later?"

Sam ended the call reluctantly, frustrated by the conversation. Every text he sent Quinn later that day resulted in one-word responses.

Sam found Ginger at their usual table on Saturday night. The band started to play, and Sam took her hand, saying, "Let's dance." They danced to several fast songs, and when the band played one of their rare slow numbers, Sam put his arms around Ginger, pulling her close. Her body was warm against his, and as much as he fought against it, he enjoyed the feel of her in his arms.

I'm only doing the same thing as Quinn.

Ginger smiled. "I thought you didn't dance."

"Six weeks ago, I didn't. Now, I do."

His friends flocked to the pool table during the band's break, but Sam sat at the table, nursing a beer while Ginger kept him company. "Trouble with the girlfriend?" she asked.

Sam snorted. "What makes you think that?"

Ginger shrugged. "You're down. You asked me to dance. It'll work out. She'd be crazy to let a great guy like you get away."

"Yeah." Sam looked at his phone. He'd gotten no messages from Quinn since late afternoon. *Maybe I need to let her know how much it hurts to not hear from her. But I'm not calling tonight.* Instead, he danced with Ginger again.

At midnight, Sam walked out the door alone. He slapped the hood of his car in frustration. *What am I doing?* When he got home, he flopped on his bed and picked up the photo strip from their last trip to Maine. Quinn was the only woman he wanted to be with. It didn't matter how nice it felt to have Ginger close to him. He shouldn't have danced with her. Had he misled her?

No. She knows I'm unavailable.

Quinn

Leigh invited Quinn to join her for lunch and they rehashed the party. "I saw you dancing with Ben from Anatomy. He's cute."

"He is, but he started grinding against me, and he was *so* sweaty." Both girls laughed, then Quinn added, "It did not thrill my boyfriend when I told him about the dancing."

"You told him? That was a mistake," Leigh said. "He can't expect you to sit in your room all the time."

"Sam isn't like that," Quinn insisted. She frowned as she remembered how she'd told Sam on the phone that Ben had *asked* her to dance.

Apparently, Leigh noticed Quinn's expression. "What's up?"

"Just thinking about how I wasn't completely truthful with Sam. But if I'd told him how Ben dragged me into dancing with him, Sam would have lost his mind." *I did the right thing.*

Sam didn't need to know that. Still, keeping something from her boyfriend made Quinn uncomfortable.

Leigh shrugged. "I'm going to a party at the Kappa house tonight. Come with me?"

Quinn shook her head. One night of feeling uncomfortable in a crowd was enough. She couldn't do two nights in a row.

Despite Quinn's refusal, Leigh grinned. "There's something going on almost every night," she said. "I'm going to keep inviting you."

Communication between Sam and Quinn continued to deteriorate. As her circle of friends increased, she spent more time with them in the early evening, which meant her homework time moved to late night when Sam wanted to talk. So many people were texting her that Sam's messages were sometimes buried or overlooked.

One Wednesday night, Sam had called late while Quinn was struggling to complete an anatomy assignment. She couldn't hide her distraction, and when he cut the call short, she told him she would be less busy on the weekend. He hadn't called again.

On Friday night, Quinn stretched out on her bed, relieved to find herself alone. She'd always considered herself an introvert, and these past days confirmed that. She had been surrounded by people all the time, and she was drained. Mason told her about another party while they were studying for Algebra the day before, and Quinn knew she would skip it. She needed time to herself.

Quinn started streaming one of her favorite shows and picked up her cell, identifying text messages she needed to delete. She reached Sam's and realized she hadn't heard from him since Thursday morning. *Over twenty-four hours. We never go that long without talking.* She'd overslept on Thursday and missed his message as she rushed to class.

I should have responded.

Quinn didn't know what to do. *I'm not interested in any of the guys I've met. They're just friends. But it's hard to stay in touch with Sam and nurture those friendships.* She frowned. *This is a new problem.* She sent Sam a text.

> Quinn: Happy Friday! I'm vegging in my room.

> Sam: No party tonight?

> Quinn: No, I need time to myself.

She held her phone, waiting for a response. After an hour went by without hearing from him, she put it down. *He's probably at that bar. I don't like this. We're on different paths.*

Finally, at midnight, her phone pinged.

> Sam: Are you awake?

> Quinn: Yes.

> Sam: Can I call? I think we need to talk.

Quinn: I think so too.

Quinn answered her ringing cell. "Hey."

"Hey." Sam paused. "I've missed talking to you."

"Me too. I got caught up with the people I've met. And the homework has gotten intense."

"Are you enjoying your new friends?"

Quinn thought about his question. "Yeah, I haven't been part of a group before. It's fun to be included."

"Anyone special in that group?"

"Are you asking if I'm interested in any of the guys?"

"Yeah. You mentioned dancing with someone. I can't help but wonder."

"I told you, that was to fill the time. There's no one special." Still, Quinn wanted to be completely honest with him. "But I've thought about what I'll do if someone acts interested in me. You know, in a dating way." She blinked back tears. "Were you attracted to anyone at Winthrop?"

"I wasn't, Quinn. You're all I want."

"There truly isn't anyone for me either, Sam. But... I guess I'm confused." She told him about her conversation with Leigh.

"I've thought about something similar." Sam's voice cracked. "What if we take a break?"

"What are you thinking?" Quinn's stomach knotted. "How long?"

"It could last until Thanksgiving, and you could spend your time however you want. You wouldn't have to worry about text messages from me or talking on the phone."

A chill went through her. "We wouldn't have any contact with each other?"

"It's killing me to wait for you to respond to my texts. And when my calls go to voicemail." Sam's voice broke again.

Tears filled Quinn's eyes. "What about you?"

"It would be the same for me. But, Quinn, I promise you that I don't plan on doing anything with another woman. I just want to give you some space."

"I need to think about it. I can't decide tonight." She wiped her cheeks. "The idea of not talking to you kills me."

"Quinn, we haven't talked since Wednesday, and the last text I sent you was thirty-six hours ago. We're already not talking."

She breathed deeply. "I'm not ready to take a formal step like that. Please keep texting me. I promise I'll respond. Let's wait a few days before we decide."

"Okay." Sam sighed. "I... I..."

"You what?"

"I can't keep not hearing from you."

"I still love you, Sam."

"And I still love you, Quinn." She could hear the emotion in his voice.

Quinn woke up to a text on Saturday.

> *Sam: Good morning, beautiful.*

She knew Sam would be happy when she responded right away.

> *Quinn: Hi, handsome. I enjoy seeing a text from you when I open my eyes.*

> *Sam: It makes my morning to hear from you.*

They continued to text the rest of the day, and that night, Sam sent her pictures of him playing pool. Sunday continued the same way.

Their discussion about a break had surprised Quinn, but she realized the turn in their relationship was confusing Sam as much as it did her. She spent the weekend in her room, doing homework, streaming television shows, and texting with Sam. It felt right.

At dinner on Sunday night, she told Leigh about their talk. Leigh responded with a grin. "Try it. You're both thinking about it. You could go wild."

"I don't think so," Quinn said. "Wild isn't in my dictionary."

"Ah, but it could be. I'll give you lessons." Leigh smirked. Quinn shook her head.

The messages slowed down on Monday and Tuesday, but Quinn knew work kept Sam busy, and she was always deep in classes at the start of the week.

As Quinn waited for Mason on Tuesday, she looked at her phone and saw that Sam had texted two hours earlier. She'd lingered in the dining hall and missed the message.

Dammit. I'm supposed to answer right away. She sent a response, but nothing came back from Sam.

A few minutes later, Mason found her staring into space. "You okay?"

She and Mason were becoming friends, and she knew he could tell she was upset. She shrugged. "I guess. I sent Sam a message, and it's been fifteen minutes without a response."

"That's really not long," Mason said gently.

"I know. It's just..." Quinn pulled her hair into a ponytail and told Mason about the conversation with Sam on Friday night.

Mason sighed. "I know what you're going through." Quinn watched as Mason rubbed his jaw, seeming hesitant about what to say. "I have a girlfriend at home. She's a senior in high school. Last year, I went home every weekend. I wasn't involved in campus life, but I didn't belong at home either. And my girlfriend wasn't as involved in her school activities as she should have been."

He twirled his pencil in his fingers. "We decided over the summer to do this year differently. I stay on campus more. I joined a fraternity, and I've made more friends here, while Penny is totally enjoying her senior year."

Quinn gazed at him. "I didn't know you had a girlfriend. You're very flirty. Do you…" She blushed. "Never mind, it's not my business what you do."

"Do I screw around?" Mason grinned at her. "No. Not yet, anyway."

"Are you going to?"

"I don't know." He grew serious. "Penny does things with her classmates. Like, she went to homecoming with the quarterback of the football team. We agree that we won't ask for details about what each other is doing." He shrugged. "Maybe I should turn in my man card, because I haven't found someone I'm interested in."

"No. You love Penny. Why should you gratuitously have sex with someone else? That's honest and real." Quinn opened her algebra book. "I love Sam, and I want to be with him. And I'm enjoying making new friends." She sighed. "I feel guilty because he's not my everything anymore."

"I get it. I felt the same way." Mason nodded. "Think about the break. It might be what you need."

After dinner, Quinn's cell finally pinged with a response from Sam. He told her he'd been in a meeting then went out to dinner with the client.

> Quinn: I feel like you're punishing me for not texting right back at noon.

> Sam: Come on, Quinn. I wouldn't do that. I had work stuff going on.

> Quinn: But you get mad at me if I don't respond right away.

She waited for a reply that didn't come. As the minutes ticked by, the knot in her stomach grew. Finally, after half an hour, her phone pinged.

> Sam: Mad isn't exactly the right word. We should talk, not text, but I've had a few drinks. I'm tired, and I'm afraid it won't go well. I'll call you tomorrow night.

Quinn digested the message. *He's been drinking. That's not my Sam.*

> Quinn: I can't tomorrow night. I'm going to a concert with Leigh.

> Sam: And I have another work thing on Thursday. Let's talk on Friday. Unless you have plans.

> Quinn: Talking to you is more important than any plans I might have.

Sam: Except for the concert tomorrow night.

Quinn: The ticket was expensive!

Sam: I get it. I'm beat. I'll talk to you on Friday.

Chapter Six

The Break

Quinn

QUINN TOOK A DEEP breath before she answered her ring-ing cell on Friday night. She knew how the conversation was going to end. "Hey."

"Hi." Sam's voice still felt familiar and comforting. "How was the concert?"

"It was good. How was your work thing?" *Good God, I'm acting like he's a stranger on the street, not the person who knows me better than anyone.*

"It was good. It's a new client for the firm, and it's going to mean a lot of business. I'm lucky they are including me in this phase."

He sounded excited. Quinn wanted to be enthusiastic, but his internship had little to do with her life. "I'm sorry I told you I thought you were punishing me. I feel like we're in very different places right now. And I don't mean me in Virginia and you in Vermont."

"I know." He sighed. "Have you thought any more about taking a break?"

"I have. Does it have to mean no contact? I'll miss you. You're my north star."

"If we keep texting and calling each other, we're going to be right where we are now. You'll get mad if I don't answer, and the same will be true for me. It's only six weeks until you come home for Thanksgiving."

"My God, Sam, that sounds like forever."

"It does for me, too, babe, but I think it's the best solution."

Quinn gazed at her poster, filled with photos of Sam. Her eyes landed on the strip from the photo booth at Old Orchard Beach. *How did we fall apart in such a short time?*

As her silence lingered, Sam asked, "Quinn, are you okay?"

"As okay as I can be. I'm remembering our time in Maine." She paused. "Should I call you when I get home for Thanksgiving?"

"Yeah."

"I fly into Burlington at nine on Wednesday night. I thought you'd pick me up."

After a moment, Sam said, "You should plan on your parents doing that."

Feeling like a dagger had plunged into her heart, Quinn struggled to find words to say to him.

Sam ended the silence. "I'm hanging up, Quinn. I'll see you at Thanksgiving." His voice broke. "I love you."

Quinn looked at the phone as their call ended. "I love you too," she whispered.

Quinn stumbled through the next several days, waiting for calls from Sam that didn't come. Every night, she held her phone and let her finger hover over the send button on a text message. Every time, she eventually put the phone down.

Dammit! I've depended on Sam since I was sixteen. He's been my everything. She took a deep breath. *I'm truly on my own now.*

A week after her last conversation with Sam, a boy Quinn didn't recognize approached the table where she was sitting with Mason and Leigh.

"Dylan!" Mason said. "Did you finally finish that mini-course?"

"Mini, my ass," the newcomer sputtered as he made his way to the open seat next to Quinn. "I worked harder in that half-semester course than in any of my full-time ones." He pulled the chair out and sat down.

Mason grinned at Quinn. "Quinn, meet Dylan."

Dylan looked at her. "You're the one pulling Mason through Algebra, kicking and screaming."

Quinn laughed, and when Dylan smiled at her, her heart fluttered. *What the hell was that?* She pushed away from the table, ready to leave for her next class.

"You should come to the party at Tau house tonight, Quinn," Mason said. "It'll be better than the first one you went to."

Leigh chimed in, urging Quinn to go.

"Okay, okay. I'll be there," Quinn said. "But right now, I have to get to my class way over on the other side of campus."

Leigh jumped up and grabbed Quinn's arm. "I have to be there early tonight. Are you okay going by yourself? If not, I can find someone to go with you."

Quinn shook her head. "I'll be fine by myself."

"You won't bail?"

"No." Quinn chuckled. "The new me wants to make herself known."

She left the dining hall, and Dylan followed her. "I'm headed to Canton Hall," he said. "Is that where you're going?"

"Yes," she managed before shyness overtook her. *Think of something to say. Come on. I talk to Mason, I talk to Ben. Why can't I talk to Dylan?*

Dylan spoke, shaking Quinn out of her stupor. "Where are you from?"

"Vermont."

"I'm from upstate New York. Are you a skier?"

Quinn perked up. Having some familiar ground to talk about made her more comfortable. "Yes, are you?"

"I am, but we won't be doing much of that around here." He turned to leave when they reached her classroom, then paused. "I'm looking forward to seeing you at the party tonight."

That evening, Quinn dressed in her favorite jeans and a pink sweater, and for the first time in a week, she didn't think about sending Sam a text. She walked out of her building and found Dylan sitting on a stone wall near the door. She cocked her head at him.

He smiled. "I asked Leigh where you lived. Hope you don't mind. Thought you might like company for the walk."

Quinn shoved her hands in her pockets. "Sure. Company would be nice."

Just like the other party, a plastic cup of punch got jammed into Quinn's hand the minute they walked in. She took a sip and choked. "This isn't any better than the first time." She looked at Dylan. "I don't drink." She put the cup down on a table.

He raised his eyebrows. "You'll be the only sober one here. That's no fun."

"It's amusing to watch everyone."

"If you say so." Dylan studied her. "Look. I'm going to have a couple of beers, and I need to speak to some people. After that, we can leave—find something else to do." He began moving toward the back of the house then stopped. "Are you coming?"

"I'll stay here," she said. "There are people I want to talk to."

"Okay. I won't be long." He cocked his head. "Don't disappear on me."

As he walked away, Quinn wondered, *Am I with him? Is this like a date? What will happen when we leave?*

She made her way over to Leigh. Ben tried to hand her another cup. She shook her head, and he said, "You need to learn to drink. Life's a lot livelier under the haze of alcohol."

Leigh chimed in, saying, "She needs something better than this swill to learn on." She leaned closer to Quinn. "You're with Dylan, huh?"

"He was waiting outside my building and walked here with me. Not sure what to call it."

"He's a flirt," Leigh said. "Don't get your hopes up for anything."

"Don't worry." *Are my hopes up? Things were a lot easier when Sam was the only one in my life.*

Dylan returned after almost an hour. Quinn was dancing with Ben, and Dylan cut in. "Let's blow this joint."

His eyes were glassy. *He's probably had more than two beers.* "What are we going to do?"

"Anything you want."

"I think I'll go back to my room." She slid him a guarded glance. "You don't need to leave with me."

"I'll walk with you."

Quinn's brow furrowed.

Dylan shook his head. "Okay. I drank more than a couple of beers, but I'm not drunk. I won't do anything you don't want. Trust me."

She wavered. *I would love to get to know him better.* Echoes of advice from her mother played in her mind. *I'll be aware of my surroundings, not let myself get backed into a dangerous situation.* "All right. If you're really okay with leaving, let's go."

As they walked side by side, Dylan asked, "What's your favorite ski mountain?"

His question surprised Quinn but having something easy to talk about made her happy. "My home mountain, of course."

"Which is?"

"Burke."

Dylan raised an eyebrow. "Wow, you're really up north. I skied there once. It was steep and fast. I ski at Whiteface."

Quinn recognized the name—it was a mountain near Lake Placid. "I've never been there."

They chatted about other places they'd skied until they reached Quinn's residence hall, and Dylan took a seat on the wall where he'd been earlier. He patted the spot beside him. "Join me. We can talk more."

She sat beside him, and they talked while they watched students staggering home from parties. The campus vibrated with groups of giggling girls, boys full of bravado, and couples walking arm in arm. *We couldn't be in a more visible place. I'm glad he didn't ask to come up to my room.*

Dylan put his arm over her shoulder and pulled her close to him. "I'd like to spend more time with you."

Quinn's heart pounded, her stomach doing cartwheels. "I'd like that too."

He leaned toward her and gently kissed her, then he stood, pulling her up and wrapping her in his arms. His hand brushed her hair. "You're beautiful." He leaned down and kissed her cheek. "Sleep tight."

Dylan let go of her and turned to leave, looking back over his shoulder. "And thanks."

"For what?"

"Saving me from a hangover." He winked and sauntered away.

Quinn went up to her room, closing her door and leaning against it. She touched her fingers to her lips. Her stomach was still doing flip-flops. Then she peeled off her clothes and put on pajama pants and a tank top before climbing onto her bed. She responded to several messages on her phone, then her thoughts wandered back to Dylan's kiss.

That was really something. Was it like that the first time Sam and I kissed?

Over the next few days, Dylan continued to show up at the dining hall and walk Quinn to her afternoon class. He always kissed her cheek as he walked away, and Quinn longed for more.

On Wednesday, the two of them went to the conference final game for the women's volleyball team. It was an exciting match, with each team taking the lead by turns. The fans on both sides of the courts were on their feet when their team spiked the ball for a two-point lead, giving them the win.

Pandemonium filled the gymnasium, and Dylan threw his arms around Quinn in excitement. "That's the way you play the game!"

The team's win made Quinn happy, but the feel of Dylan's body against hers surpassed the thrill of the victory. He released her, and they exited the gym, crushed together in the crowd.

Dylan suggested they stop for ice cream. Quinn ordered a sundae with hot fudge, and Dylan got one with butterscotch. They were almost done eating when he surprised her by holding his spoon to her lips. Butterscotch dripped from it, and his eyes twinkled, challenging her to open her mouth. She did so happily, savoring the sweetness of both the sauce and his gesture.

Chapter Seven

Ginger's Apartment

Sam

THE DAY AFTER HE and Quinn decided to take the break, Sam split logs all day, relieved to have a distraction to keep him away from his cell. He knew he'd been cruel, refusing to pick her up and ending the call abruptly, but he couldn't keep going the way they had been.

He left the forest sweaty and physically exhausted.

I could easily stay home tonight, but I don't want to be alone. I'll check for a text from Quinn every five minutes, even though I told her no contact.

Jilly and Ginger were sitting with Quinn's friends Casey and Julie when Sam and Matt walked into the Whistle Stop. Sam sat beside Ginger, who greeted him with a warm smile. Julie asked, "Are you counting the days until Quinn comes home? I miss her so much—I can't wait to see her. You must be going crazy."

Sam shrugged. "Something like that."

The table emptied as people left to play pool or to dance. Sam drained his beer bottle, and the server slid him another one. He had added a second beer to his evenings at the bar around the time Quinn started being distant. *Maybe I'll go wild and have three tonight.*

After a moment, Sam looked up to see Ginger watching him.

"Did you talk to Quinn?" she asked.

Sam nodded. He had seen Ginger at the bar on Wednesday night and told her he and Quinn were thinking about a break. Ginger had enthusiastically told him about a couple who had taken a month-long break that made them realize the depth of their love. She said they were getting married on Valentine's Day. Sam hoped that would happen for him and Quinn.

"How did it go?"

"It went okay. We're not going to have any contact until she comes home for Thanksgiving." He fiddled with the label on the beer bottle. "She said there's no one she's interested in dating, and I told her I felt the same way."

"You're free to date if someone comes along. That's the point of a break."

"Yeah, I don't see that happening. Not for me anyway." Sam felt hollow inside as he watched his friends enjoying themselves.

Ginger reached over and stroked his arm. "I don't like seeing you so dejected. You shouldn't be put through this. She won't find anyone any better."

Sam didn't respond. He finished his beer and realized he didn't want to be there. "I'm heading home. I worked in the woods all day, and I'm beat."

"It's supposed to rain tomorrow. You won't work outside in that, will you?"

Sam shook his head.

Ginger smiled. "Come over to my apartment and watch movies with me. You shouldn't spend the day alone. You'll wonder what she's doing."

Uncertain, Sam rubbed the back of his neck and thought about Ginger's offer. "Are you positive you don't mind being a diversion for me?" *Don't do it. This will lead to trouble,* his conscience screamed.

"Not at all, Sam." Ginger leaned closer. "I understand what it's like to need a friend. My door's open any time."

Sam arrived at Ginger's place in mid-afternoon, and they watched a comedy. He laughed more than he had since Quinn left, and when the movie ended, Ginger suggested they order a pizza and watch another. Sam ended up staying until after ten.

As he opened the door to leave, Ginger asked, "Do you want to come over tomorrow night?" She tugged free the band holding her ponytail and shook out her hair. "It would be a break from being at the bar every night."

Sam leaned against the doorjamb, lost in thought. "Yeah, that might be good. It's rough, sitting at the Whistle and watching all the couples."

At home, he stretched out on his bed with his phone in hand, gazing at the screen, wishing a text from Quinn would appear.

You told her no contact. Did you think she would do something different?

He spent his evenings the rest of that week either watching movies at Ginger's apartment or hanging out with his friends at the Whistle Stop. Ginger didn't seem to expect anything from him, which was a relief.

Every night, he fought the urge to text Quinn.

Sam opened his eyes in unfamiliar surroundings. *What the hell?*

He struggled to a sitting position, looking around the dimly lit room, and the night before came rushing back to him. It had been a week since he'd told Quinn they should take a break, and he'd joined his coworkers for drinks after work before going to Ginger's apartment. The previous times he'd visited Ginger, he'd sat in her recliner to watch television, but when he arrived that night, it had been filled with laundry.

Ginger apologized and started to move the clothes. Sam told her to stop, that the couch offered plenty of room for both of them. They'd sat at opposite ends, Ginger curling her legs under her and giving Sam room to stretch out.

I must have passed out. She covered me up and went to bed. He scrubbed his hands over his face. *I need to stop coming over here. She should spend time with guys who will show her more fun.*

He wondered how Quinn had spent Friday night. God, he missed her.

Silently, he made his way out of Ginger's apartment, but before he started his car, he sent her a text of apology. He ended it with, *your couch is too comfortable,* and a smiling emoji.

On Saturday night, Julie went up to Sam at the bar and confronted him. "You spent last night with Ginger? I know you and Quinn are on a break, but really, Sam—it's only been a week!"

He took a step back from her. "Whoa, whoa, whoa. I didn't *spend* the night with Ginger. I fell asleep watching a movie. She threw a blanket over me and went to bed. By herself. I woke up in the middle of the night and went home."

Julie frowned. "That's not the picture Ginger is painting."

Sam sighed. "I'll talk to her." He took a swallow of his beer. "Have you heard from Quinn?"

Julie nodded.

"How is she?" he asked.

"She's okay. The schoolwork is challenging."

"Has she mentioned… you know, going out with any-one?" Sam was haunted by the thought of Quinn with an-other man.

Julie looked pointedly at him. "She hasn't slept in some-one else's room."

Sam grimaced. "Give me a break, Julie. It wasn't like that."

She raised her eyebrows.

"Do me a favor? Don't tell Quinn. Please."

Before she could answer, Casey pulled Julie to the dance floor, leaving Sam by himself. He walked over to Ginger, who sat alone at their usual table. "Are you telling people we slept together?"

She shook her head, looking surprised. "No, of course not. Where'd you get that idea?"

He gritted his teeth. "From Julie."

"She misunderstood me, Sam." She held up her hands, palms out. "I told Jilly how cute you looked on my couch. I know you're not looking for anything like that."

Sam's jaw tightened. "You need to set it right with Julie. I don't need Quinn's best friend thinking I'm sleeping with someone."

Sam sat down, and when Julie came back, Ginger leaned toward her. "Did you hear Sam fell asleep on my couch? Can't you just imagine how much he loved sleeping under a pink leopard-print blanket?"

When Sam rose to leave, Julie jumped up and followed him. She grabbed his arm and leaned toward him. "You can't trust her."

Sam stopped. "Ginger explained what happened. And it was exactly the same as what I told you."

"I don't trust her," Julie insisted, "and you shouldn't either."

"She knows about Quinn." Sam rubbed his jaw. "I had the same thought, Julie—that Ginger might be looking for something more. I hesitated about spending time with her. But I'm lonely, and she's been nothing but a friend."

"You think Quinn's not lonely? She's a thousand miles away, surrounded by total strangers!"

"She's making friends. So many friends that she doesn't have time for me. That's why we're taking a break."

"She still loves you, Sam. You know that."

Sam sighed. "I don't know much these days, Julie. Not much at all."

The next weekend, Sam paced back and forth, guzzling his beer and trying to beat back his frustration with his father while he watched Matt playing pool. He and Matt had worked all day for the man, but apparently that wasn't enough. Sam had almost been out the door on his way to the Whistle Stop when his father stopped him, saying, "I need your help tomorrow at that house on Main Street."

Sam couldn't spend another day with his father. "Sorry, Dad. I have plans tomorrow."

"Plans? You have plans? Do your *plans* include paying rent to your mother and me? Because that's our agreement. You live in this house rent-free and do the jobs I give you. Should we renegotiate that?"

Sam knew his father was drinking and would probably forget the entire conversation by morning. Regardless, Sam intended to be somewhere else.

Watching the pool match did nothing to ease his irritation, and when Ginger walked in, Sam grabbed her hand and dragged her to the dance floor. He kept her there until the band took a break.

Back at the table, he took a long swallow of his beer and drummed his fingers, still feeling restless.

"You're in a mood," Ginger said. "Did something happen between you and Quinn?"

Sam scoffed. "What's going to happen? We agreed to having no contact with each other. It's been two weeks, and you know what? It's actually getting easier." He drained his bottle. "It's my dad. Matt and I gave him our whole Saturday, and now he wants tomorrow too. I'm tired of it."

Ginger signaled the server to bring another round of drinks, then put her hand on top of Sam's. "What are you going to do?"

"Make myself scarce tomorrow. Although I'm not exactly sure where I'm going."

Ginger ran her hand up Sam's arm. "You could..." She paused there.

"What? I could what?" His nostrils flared. He wasn't in the mood to play Twenty Questions. "Just spit it out, Ginger."

"Never mind. It's a dumb idea."

Sam cocked his head, silently urging her to tell him her thoughts.

Ginger shrugged. "You could stay at my place tonight and hang around tomorrow, watching movies. We know you can fall asleep on my couch." She flashed him a conspiratorial smile.

Sam thought for a moment. "You wouldn't mind?"

She shook her head.

Julie's words from the week before echoed in his head. *Fuck it. I trust Ginger. She's being a good friend.* "A break from my dad would be welcome," he said.

The band started, and they danced again. After several fast songs, the tempo changed to slow and sultry. Sam pulled Ginger close, and she nestled her head on his chest.

"I had a rough week, and I'm exhausted," Ginger said when they were back at the table during the band's next break. "I'm going home. If you want to stay at my apartment, come over after you leave here. I'll probably be in bed, but I'll leave the door unlocked for you." She covered a yawn while she shrugged on her jacket.

"Nah, I'll leave too. What will I do without my dance partner?"

At her apartment, Ginger locked the door behind Sam and retrieved a pillow and blanket from her bedroom closet. She placed them on the couch and gave her head an exaggerated shake. "My ears are ringing from the band. Would you mind if I have a glass of wine?"

Sam leaned against the wall. "It's your place, Ginger. Why would I mind if you have a drink? Let's watch a couple of episodes of that show we started last week."

Ginger returned to the living room with a beer for Sam and wine for herself. They sat together on the couch, as the recliner was full of laundry again. Ginger edged closer to him, and Sam felt awkward with his arm between them, so he laid it over the back of the sofa, lightly touching her shoulders. After the second episode of their show ended, they both leaned forward to put their glasses on the coffee table. They laughed as their foreheads came together.

After a moment's pause, Ginger leaned in and gently kissed Sam. She gazed at him. "Surprise."

Sam studied her for a second before leaning in to return the kiss. Their arms went around each other, and heat rose quickly between them. Sam leaned back against the pillow Ginger had placed on the couch earlier, pulling her along to lie on top of him.

They continued kissing, and she slid her hand between them, slowly moving it down. When her fingers came to the bulge in his pants, Sam eased her away from him. "I'm sorry," he said. "I know that wasn't what you invited me here for, and it wasn't what I came for."

"Sam, I like you. I don't mind, and I don't have any expectations."

He shook his head. "No, I won't take advantage of you that way." He stood. "I should go home."

Ginger got to her feet and put her hand on Sam's arm. "No, please stay. I shouldn't have kissed you, knowing things with Quinn are up in the air. I'm going to bed. Really, stay—it's fine." She walked into her bedroom and closed the door.

Shit. I don't feel that way about her. Or I didn't think I did. She's fun to hang out with, but I don't know what will happen with Quinn at Thanksgiving.

He sat back down on the couch. *I'll stay tonight but leave in the morning and see what Dad wants.* He ran his fingers through his hair. *Has this been Ginger's long game? Have I been a fool?*

Quinn and I didn't play games like this.

Sam stayed home for several nights after the make out session with Ginger. He realized Julie had been right—Ginger couldn't be trusted—but the truth was that he'd enjoyed her kisses. He spent most of that week trying to figure out what he was going to do at Thanksgiving. He loved Quinn and missed her, but he wasn't as sure about marrying her as he'd once been. At least not without exploring things with Ginger first.

On Friday, snow started falling, and a text from Philippe surprised Sam that evening.

> Phillippe: I'm on my way to visit Sylvie but can't keep driving in this snow. You said stop anytime. How about now?

> Sam: Yes!

Sam took Philippe to the Whistle Stop. They picked up beers at the bar and went to the pool table. "Aha, you've started drinking beer! And how is the beautiful Quinn? How many times have you made that long drive?"

Sam shrugged. "I spend most of my free time here. Drinking comes with the territory." He handed Philippe a pool cue. "Quinn and I are taking a break."

"*Mais non!*" Philippe frowned. "What happened?"

"She's busy with new friends. It was too hard to stay in touch."

Phillipe gave him a look. "Work at it and have patience. You think it was easy for Sylvie and me? You give up too easily."

After playing pool, Sam took Philippe to his usual table and introduced him, running quickly through everyone's names. Ginger took Sam's arm and nodded toward the dance floor.

He pulled back. "Not tonight. I haven't seen Philippe since August."

The next morning, the sky was bright blue, and the roads were clear. Sam helped Philippe brush off his car, and before his friend left, Sam clapped him on the back. "Give Sylvie a hug for me."

"I'll give her many hugs and tell her one is from you." Philippe laughed then shook his head. "That girl, Ginger? She's after you. Be careful."

Chapter Eight

Dylan

Quinn

ON SATURDAY, QUINN STARED at the text from her best friend.

> Julie: Sam hangs out with this girl named Ginger at the Whistle Stop. They dance and he goes to her apartment to watch movies. Last week, she told everyone that he spent the night with her. I asked him about it, and he said he fell asleep watching a movie and left in the middle of the night. I thought you should know.

> *Quinn: Which one of them is telling the truth?*

> *Julie: I confronted Sam, and he was shaken. Ginger said it was innocent, but I don't trust her.*

Quinn frowned. That last text from Julie hadn't exactly answered her question. Quinn knew Sam had the same right as she did to hang out with other people. *The time I spend with Dylan isn't any different.*

She spread her books out on the bed and tried to study, but thoughts of Dylan and Sam kept intruding. Sam was the only man she'd ever been with. They dated over a year before they had sex. He was her first kiss and her first sexual experience, and Quinn loved him with all her heart. She believed sex should express love and wasn't something to go into casually. And she'd thought Sam felt the same way. But Julie's story raised questions. Maybe Sam didn't feel that way anymore.

Do I still feel that way?

Quinn's thoughts drifted to Wednesday night. After the sundaes, as they walked toward her residence hall, she and Dylan had passed a park bench. "Let's sit," he'd said. The bench was more secluded than the wall where they'd sat before, and Quinn wondered what would happen.

Dylan had put his arm over Quinn's shoulders, pulling her close to him. He turned and lowered his lips to hers, more aggressively this time. His tongue pressed insistently against her lips, and she opened her mouth, willingly inviting him in. After a few minutes, they stood, and he wrapped his arms around her, thrusting his hips against her, his erection obvious. The heat she felt between her legs increased as they clung to each other, then he let her go, stroking her hair the same way he had after the party.

Back at her residence hall, Dylan had given her a suggestive look. "Want to invite me in?" When Quinn shook her head, he chuckled. "That's what I was afraid of." He had ducked his head and kissed her cheek before he left.

Her mind returned to Julie's text, and she picked up her phone again.

> *Quinn: I'm not falling asleep in his room, but I've been hanging out with this guy named Dylan. We're going to a party tonight.*

That night, Dylan was waiting for her on the wall, and Quinn broke into a huge smile when she saw him. She ran over to lean down and kiss him. "I've been looking forward to seeing you all day."

He put his arm over her shoulder, bringing her close to him, as they walked to the party and went inside. "Have you changed your mind about drinking?"

"No." Quinn shook her head and watched as Dylan downed a beer before leading her to the dance floor. The music featured a pounding techno beat, and Quinn was gasping for breath by the time a slower song finally played. She wrapped her arms around Dylan and rested her head on his chest. As they swayed together, he nibbled on her neck, and Quinn sighed with pleasure.

"One of my friends has a room here," Dylan said. "We could have some alone time."

Quinn gasped. "I don't know about that."

They continued swaying to the music, Dylan holding her against him. "We won't do anything you don't want to do." His mouth met hers, bringing the same heat that she'd felt after the volleyball game. "Please? I won't hurt you, Quinn."

She raised her head to whisper in his ear, "I'm not ready to go all the way with you."

"That's okay. I wish you were, but I'll respect what you want." He kissed her again. "There are other things we can do."

Quinn hesitated then let him lead her up the stairs to a small bedroom. *I hope this isn't a mistake.*

Dylan closed the door behind them. "I'm not locking the door. You're free to leave if that's what you want, I promise. I will not hurt you."

"I trust you." Quinn ran her fingers along his jawbone and stood on her tiptoes to kiss him.

"I know you don't drink, but how about getting stoned?"

Her eyes widened. "I don't do that either." She hoped he could hear the shock in her tone. She stepped closer to him, took his hands, and gazed into his eyes. "I don't need to be drunk or high to spend time with you."

"I'm glad." Dylan tugged one hand free and slid it under her sweater, stroking the skin of her back. "So soft," he breathed. "I knew your skin would feel just like this. Tell me if you want me to stop."

"I will."

The room was small, and they were only steps from the bed. Dylan crossed the distance, sitting on the edge of the mattress and pulling Quinn into his lap. He shifted his hand around to her breasts, caressing her bra and eventually sliding his fingers inside. "Let's lay down," he whispered.

In answer, Quinn slipped off his lap, laying her head on the pillow and beckoning him to join her. Dylan laid on his side and pulled her to him. His hips swiveled against her, and Quinn felt the bulge she knew would be there. She stroked him, and it brought back memories. *I did this all the time with Sam that first year. How far are we going to go? I don't want to jerk him off, but he'll probably be pissed if I don't.* She jumped at the feel of his hand between her legs, stroking her where she most wanted it.

They continued teasing each other until Dylan stopped and put some distance between them. "I knew this would be outstanding. Are you a virgin?"

Quinn shook her head vigorously.

"So why are you reluctant to go all the way? We're both ready." He reached his hand between her legs again.

Quinn moaned and thrust against his hand. "I've only known you for two weeks. It doesn't seem long enough for… that." Still, she moved her hand to his erection again. The heat escalated between them, and she considered unzipping his jeans.

Dylan groaned in frustration and climbed off the bed. "Let's leave. I need to cool down." He reached his hand out to help her up. They left the house and started across the campus, walking side by side without touching or talking.

When they reached her building, he asked, "I suppose you still won't ask me in?"

Quinn shook her head, and Dylan kissed her cheek. He stepped back, looking like he wanted to say something, but only shook his head before kissing Quinn's cheek once again and walking away.

When she went inside, Quinn was surprised to see Wendy in their room. "Have you been crying?"

Wendy shrugged. "A little. We had a fight. We'll get over it." She smirked. "I don't need to ask what you've been doing. You look like you've been ravished."

"Not ravished enough, in Dylan's opinion. I'm not ready to have sex with him yet, and I don't think he's happy about it."

On Monday, Quinn was surprised when Dylan showed up to walk her to her afternoon class. "I wasn't sure I'd see you again," she admitted.

"You're going to be worth the wait." Instead of kissing her cheek, he gathered her into a hug and kissed her lips. "I'll be ready when you are."

Quinn tingled inside every time she thought of Dylan's words. *I thought Sam was one of a kind, but I've found someone else like him. He's patient and not pushing me for more than I'm ready to give.*

While Quinn studied with Mason on Tuesday, he seemed subdued. He solved an equation before Quinn, and when she high-fived him in congratulations, his only response was a grunt.

"What's wrong with you? We've only got a few weeks left in the semester, and you are doing great. I expected more excitement."

After a moment of silence, Mason put his hand on Quinn's arm. "Just... be careful."

Quinn raised her eyebrows.

"With Dylan, I mean," he added. "He's a good friend, the first one I made here last year, but I don't want you to expect more than he's going to give."

"I'm not expecting anything." Quinn smiled. "You're sweet to worry about me, but Dylan's been great. I should be thanking you for introducing us."

Mason nodded but frowned. "I don't want to see you get hurt."

"I'll be fine."

Two days later, Sylvie sent Quinn a text, telling her she was in Washington, DC, and wanted to visit Quinn for lunch.

When Sylvie arrived, Quinn threw her arms around her. "I'm so happy to see someone from home. Well, almost home. I think about the summer all the time."

"*Moi aussi!* Me too. How is that sweet boy, Sam?"

"I haven't talked to him in over three weeks." Tears welled in Quinn's eyes. Seeing Sylvie brought memories of the summer rushing back, and Quinn wondered again how her relationship with Sam could have unraveled so quickly. *I miss him.* "We're taking a break."

Sylvie shook her head. "Philippe stayed with Sam last weekend and he told me this, but I didn't believe it. You were good together."

Quinn told her their communication had become difficult and that they seemed to have little in common these days.

"Philippe gave Sam some good advice, and I will tell you the same. You need to try harder."

They walked around the campus, and Quinn smiled when she saw Dylan coming toward them. His eyes lit up, and he stopped in front of them. "I missed you at lunch," he said.

"My friend Sylvie stopped to visit." Quinn introduced them.

After talking a few minutes with them, Dylan said, "I need to head to class." He put his hands on Quinn's shoulders and leaned in to kiss her cheek before walking away.

Quinn turned back to Sylvie. "Don't look at me like that."

"Like what?" Sylvie feigned innocence.

"Like I'm doing something wrong!" Quinn jammed her hands into her pockets. "The whole point of the break is to let me figure out what I want. I can't do that in a vacuum."

"You sleep with him?"

"No!" Quinn blushed. "Not yet anyway." When Sylvie shook her head, Quinn asked, "Is Philippe the only man you've been with?"

"No. I didn't meet him until just before I left for university. I had boyfriends in high school."

"And you had sex with them?"

"A few, yes."

"Sam is the only boyfriend I've ever had. I'd never even kissed another boy. Until I met Dylan."

Sylvie nodded and took Quinn's hands. "I understand. But I worry about you being hurt. College men can be players. And Philippe told me there is a woman after Sam."

Quinn grimaced. "I know. I've heard about her."

Before Sylvie got in her car to drive back to Washington, she kissed both of Quinn's cheeks. "You have a good thing with Sam. I don't want to see you lose it."

At lunch on Friday, Dylan asked Quinn, "Are you going to save me from a hangover tomorrow night?" When she gave him an inquisitive look, he added, "If you spend the evening with me, then I won't feel obligated to go to that party Mason mentioned."

Quinn laughed, feeling a little nervous. "What are you thinking?"

"There's a Marvel movie showing in the student center. I'll meet you at our wall for the walk over."

Our wall. His words made Quinn tingle.

Chapter Nine

Quinn's Missteps

Quinn

THERE'S LESS THAN TWO weeks left until Thanksgiving.

Quinn squeezed into her favorite jeans and thought about the night ahead of her. *How long will Dylan wait for me? I feel like I'm being a tease. He turns me on, and truthfully, I'm curious about what it's like with someone else.* She pulled a sweater over her head. *I'll see where the evening goes and not hold back.*

Quinn studied her face in the mirror. She flicked a mascara wand over her eyelashes and thought about Sam. Julie and Sylvie had both warned her he was spending time with a girl at that bar. *How far is he taking it with her?* She stroked blush over her cheekbones.

It doesn't matter. Whatever I do, I'm doing it for myself.

The movie was over before ten. "Damn, that ended too early," Dylan said as they left the student center. "I may not avoid that hangover after all. Unless... I'd like to see the movie that preceded this one. Do you have streaming?"

Quinn nodded.

"Could we watch in your room?"

She missed a step. "Sure."

In her room, Quinn found a note from Wendy saying she had gone home for the night. When she showed it to Dylan, his mouth curled into a smile. "So, we're alone." He reached out his arms. "Come here." She walked into his embrace, and he lowered his lips to hers. "Which bed is yours?"

Quinn was sure Dylan could feel her heart pounding. "Are we even going to pretend to watch the movie?"

"Will that make you more comfortable?"

"No." Quinn toggled on her desk lamp and flipped a switch, turning off the overhead light. "We don't need it so bright in here." With her heart still nearly jumping out of her chest, she took his hand and led him to her bed, sitting with her legs dangling over the edge. She opened them, inviting him to come closer.

Dylan stepped between her thighs, which Quinn wrapped around him, before lowering her lips to his. She patted the mattress. "Come here."

Dylan climbed up beside her and slid his hands under her sweater. He fondled her breasts, and Quinn moaned in response. He shoved her sweater up and dipped his mouth to her lacy bra.

Quinn inched her hands toward his erection, and when she reached it, Dylan drew in a breath. He moved away from her. "Are you ready to have sex with me tonight? Because if we go much further, I won't be able to stop."

"I... think so."

"That's not good enough, sweetheart." He guided Quinn's hand back to the bulge in his jeans. "Feel that? It's how much I want you. If we're not going all the way, we need to stop now."

Quinn stroked his erection. "I don't want to stop."

"I've been waiting to hear that since the moment I met you." He grasped the hem of her sweater and tugged it over her head then shoved her bra down, taking her nipple in his mouth and sucking aggressively.

Quinn moaned and fumbled with his zipper.

"So hot," Dylan murmured. "You are so hot. I can't wait to be inside you." He unzipped his jeans and pushed them off. He guided Quinn back to his erection. "That's all for you. Take your jeans off, sweetheart."

Quinn shimmied them off, and Dylan groaned at the sight of her thong. He hooked his fingers into it, yanked it off, and climbed on top of her.

"Wait a minute," she said. "You need a condom."

"Seriously? Aren't you on the Pill or an IUD?"

Before then, he'd been talking to her in the soft, sexy voice that Quinn loved, but this harsh response to her comment about using a condom startled her. *Yes, I'm on the Pill, but I'm not having unprotected sex with someone I've known for less than a month.* She pointed at the stand beside her bed. *Even after a year, Sam and I still used condoms. Double protection.* "There are condoms in that drawer."

Dylan opened the drawer and removed a foil packet then looked at Quinn. "You bring guys here often?"

"No." She felt her face flush. "You know I'm involved with someone at home—he's visited. It's complicated."

"There's nothing complicated about me. I think you're smoking hot, and I want you." He shoved his boxers to the floor and climbed back onto the bed beside her. Taking her hand, he wrapped it around his erection. "That's what you do to me."

Quinn stroked him while he opened the packet, then he moved her hand aside and rolled the condom on. Dylan's lips crushed Quinn's, and he leaned against her, pushing her flat on the bed. His body covered hers, and he nudged her legs apart.

He rubbed his cock against her slit, and his lips moved from her mouth down to her breast where he nipped at her pink nubs. He hadn't even taken off his shirt.

My God, this couldn't be any more different from Sam. He's always tender and playful. It's exciting in a totally different way.

She waited for him to touch her some more, maybe slide a finger in, but without more pretext, Dylan entered her roughly, moving furiously. His weight restrained her, and Quinn struggled to catch her breath. *A little more foreplay would have been nice.* She was dry, and his thrusts were uncomfortable. *I don't think I'm going to come.* She pretended to be into it, hoping he would finish soon.

Dylan's strokes became faster, and he orgasmed with a groan, collapsing onto Quinn, making it even harder for her to breathe.

She tried unsuccessfully to wiggle out from under him. "Dylan, I can't move."

He rolled off and lay beside her, panting. He finally sat up and kissed Quinn on the cheek before getting off the bed to go to the bathroom. When he came back, he pulled on his boxers and jeans then jammed his feet into his sneakers.

Quinn wrapped the blanket around her and sat up. "Are you leaving?" She tried not to sound needy.

Dylan picked up his jacket and shrugged it on. "I don't stay overnight." With that and a wave, he left.

Not even a goodbye? That was the definition of "Wham, bam, thank you, ma'am." Quinn touched a finger to her sore mouth. *Except he didn't even say thank you.*

What did I do?

Slowly, Quinn climbed off the bed, walked to the bathroom, and stepped into the shower, turning the water to its hottest setting. She scrubbed every inch of her body. After she toweled off, she gazed at her face in the mirror and shook her head.

Now I know what it's like with another guy. Not that great.

Quinn woke up Sunday morning to a text from Leigh inviting her to brunch.

> **Leigh: If your head feels better, you should come!**

If my head feels better? What the hell is she talking about?

Quinn replied, saying she'd meet Leigh at eleven.

As soon as Quinn sat down at the restaurant, she began to question Leigh. "What do you think is wrong with my head?"

"Dylan showed up at the party last night and said you had a migraine. Those are brutal."

Quinn sat back in her chair, her body heating as she processed this. Of course Dylan had lied. "I don't think I said migraine, but whatever. I'm fine. Did he stay long at the party?"

"He got rip-roaringly drunk. Mason had to make sure he got back to his room. What happened before he split?"

Quinn's face flushed. "We saw the movie at the student center and then went to my room to watch another one."

"Your room—*ooh la la*. Just to watch a movie?" Leigh grinned provocatively.

"Something like that." Quinn saw no point in sharing anything else. "I'm going to get some ice cream. Do you want any?"

The line was long, and while Quinn waited, she considered Dylan lying about her having a migraine. Then she heard a girl behind her say "Dylan," and she turned her head, trying to follow the conversation without being obvious. *Is she talking about my Dylan?*

"We get together," the girl was saying, "but he's chasing after this freshman girl."

"So what are you?" her friend asked. "On hold?"

The girl laughed. "I wouldn't call it that. He spent the night with me on Friday. Last night, he had a movie date with the freshman."

My God, she is *talking about me!*

"Not sure how it went, though," the girl continued, "because his roommate told me Dylan's nursing a massive hangover this morning."

Quinn's ears began to ring. *He was with someone else the night before we were together.* Nausea overtook her.

Dylan intercepted Quinn on the walk to her afternoon class on Monday. "Hi, sweetheart." He slung an arm over her shoulder, drawing her to his side.

Quinn ducked out from under his arm, putting distance between them. "You don't need to walk me to class."

"I like to." Dylan made a move toward her, but Quinn stepped off the walkway onto the grass. Dylan stopped and raised his hands in surrender. "Okay, message received. I enjoy being with you, Quinn."

"Really?" Quinn tried and failed to keep her tone civil. "Then why did you bolt out of my room on Saturday night?"

"Is that what you're mad about? It's always awkward after the first time. I figured you'd want time to yourself to process things."

"I figured maybe you wanted to go back to the girl you were with on Friday night."

"Friday night?" Dylan's steps slowed but Quinn kept going. "What are you talking about?"

"A tall blond who spent Friday night with *Dylan* but couldn't see him Saturday night because he had a movie date with the freshman girl he's after. Ring any bells?"

"I don't know what you expect, Quinn, but I'm not looking to be exclusive. We have fun together, but I have fun with other people too."

They reached Quinn's classroom, and she turned to face him with her hands on her hips. "I'm not interested in being with someone who fucks around and expects to have unprotected sex with me the next day. Please stay away from me. You were a big mistake."

Dylan shrugged. "Have it your way. But those are my friends you hang out with. You're going to see me around."

"Thanks for the warning. I'll find different friends." Quinn walked into her classroom and sat down, trying to control her trembling body while she fought off tears of anger.

Quinn spent the week thinking about the guys she'd met at school. They told jokes and made crude remarks about women. They were all obsessed with sex, but there was no feeling behind it.

I know now that's not what I want. Sam loves me and always treats me well. I love him, and I want the life we've been talking about.

The biggest question was the best way to tell Sam she wanted to end the break. She would be going home for Thanksgiving in one week, but she couldn't wait. *I need to talk to him before that.*

And I'm not telling him I had sex with Dylan. That's getting buried, and I hope eventually I can just forget it ever happened.

That night, Quinn's phone pinged with a text from Julie.

Julie: Anything else with Dylan?

Quinn hesitated, but Julie was her closest friend. She could trust Julie with her secret, and it would be good to tell somebody.

Quinn: This is just between us. Pinky swear?

Julie: Of course.

Quinn: I had sex with him Saturday night.

Julie: Whoa!

Quinn: Yeah—it sucked, and I discovered he's an asshole. I'm going to let Sam know I want to end this stupid break.

Julie: That wasn't what I expected to hear.

Quinn: Sam's the one for me. I can't wait to come home. I don't want him to know what happened with Dylan, so please, please, keep this secret.

Chapter Ten

Sam's Missteps

Sam

On Friday night, Sam walked into the Whistle Stop, smiling when he saw Ginger. They went to the dance floor, and he hoped for a slow one so they could be close. His wish came true on the fourth song, and he wrapped his arms around Ginger, drawing her to him.

The band took a break, and he whispered in her ear, "Can we go outside? I want to talk privately." Ginger nodded, and he grabbed her coat as they headed outside. They walked to his car, and Sam eased her arms into her coat. "I don't want you to be cold." He fingered the buttons on the coat. "I don't know..." he began.

Then he gazed into her eyes, and the desire to hold her overcame him. He opened his arms. "Come here." Ginger stepped closer, and Sam covered her mouth with his.

She melted against him. "I won't be cold with you doing this."

Out of the corner of his eye, Sam saw Julie and Casey approaching. His arms dropped to his sides and he backed away from Ginger. "Great."

"Brrrr. It's chilly out here." Julie pulled Casey to a stop. "I bet Quinn's a lot warmer in Virginia." She smirked as she looked from Sam to Ginger. "Don't you think so, Sam?"

Sam clenched his fists and took a deep breath. "Probably."

"I hope she brings a coat when she comes home on Wednesday." Julie winked at Sam. "But maybe it won't matter because she'll have you to keep her warm."

Sam remained quiet. *I've never hit a woman and I never will but oh, do I want to wipe that smile off Julie's face.*

Casey shot him a sympathetic look.

Julie turned her gaze toward Ginger. "You don't know Quinn, do you?"

Ginger remained silent as Sam watched Julie's eyes shooting sparks toward her.

"You'll get to meet her next week. I'm sure Sam will bring her here since it's his favorite place to hang out." Julie's eyes moved back to Sam. "Right?"

"Let's head in, Jules." Casey clamped his hand on her arm and started walking toward the door.

Julie turned her head back to Sam. "Aren't you coming in with us?"

Sam watched Casey whisper in Julie's ear and heard her laughter as they walked away. He turned away from Ginger, trying to control the anger that had started bubbling inside him as soon as Julie started talking. He put his hands on the roof of his car and took several deep breaths before turning back to Ginger. "I'm sorry about that. I'll never understand why she and Quinn are such good friends."

"I'm a big girl. I can take it. Do you want to go back in?" She placed her hand on his cheek. "Or do you want to tell me whatever it is we came out here for?"

Sam wrapped his arms around Ginger and held her tightly, still trying to get his temper under control. Finally, he moved his lips to her mouth, letting his anger turn to passion.

Reluctantly, Sam ended the kiss then ran his fingers through her hair. "You're hard to resist." He grasped her tightly against him before pulling away and putting his hands on Ginger's shoulders. "Look, I don't know what's going to happen when Quinn comes home. We need to figure out where things stand between us. I won't have sex with you until that is settled. But if you want to—well, I wouldn't mind more of this."

"I'd love more of this." She traced her fingers across his lips. "Do you want to go to my apartment?"

"You're sure you understand things could go either way with Quinn?" Ginger nodded. "Okay, then. I'd like to go to your apartment."

Sam followed Ginger to her apartment and sat in his car for a few minutes, still trying to corral his emotions. He pictured Quinn in the bell tower during his last night in Virginia, her face glowing like the setting sun after he told her he wanted them to be engaged. And, of course, the engagement ring he'd ordered with such anticipation had been delivered before he and Quinn decided to take a break.

Initially, Sam had placed it on his nightstand where he could see it and envision getting down on one knee, saying the magic words to Quinn, then sliding the ring onto her finger. As his attraction to Ginger had grown, the ring had mocked him as he crawled into bed every night. Finally, the day after Philippe's visit, with his admonition to "try harder" ringing in Sam's ears, he had snatched the ring off the nightstand and jammed it under some clothes. He hadn't looked at it since, his socks and boxers shielding it from his sight.

Sam looked at Ginger, who stood expectantly in her doorway. *I still love Quinn, but I have to figure out what this is.* Blowing out the breath he'd been holding, he got out of the car.

Ginger opened her arms to Sam as he climbed the stairs to her door. She tugged him inside and held him the same way he had held her in the parking lot. "I wish Julie hadn't gotten you all stirred up."

"Me too," Sam snorted. "Just give me a few minutes." He kept his arms around Ginger.

She stepped back from him, unzipped his jacket and reached for the lapels, trying to slide it off his shoulders. When Sam took over and shrugged it off, Ginger removed her own coat and tossed it on top of Sam's.

Ginger placed her hands on Sam's chest and slid them down to his belt. Sam's cock hardened as her hands worked, the confrontation with Julie moving to the back of his mind. Once the belt was unbuckled, Ginger's hand moved over the obvious bulge in his jeans.

Sam groaned in response to her touch, and Ginger dropped to her knees in front of him. She undid the button and then moved to the zipper. As she gripped his jeans and boxers, shoving them to the floor, his cock sprung free.

Ginger looked up at Sam, smiled briefly, then enveloped his erection with her mouth. With rational thought pushed from his mind, Sam thrust against her. Her hands cradled his balls, and her mouth moved in and out on his cock.

Sam's hands reached for her hair and stilled her motion. "You're killing me. We shouldn't..."

Ginger looked up at him again. "I want to."

The persistent buzzing of his cell woke Sam on Saturday morning. Sam and Ginger had made out late into the night, stopping shy of intercourse but with both of them bringing the other to climax with their mouths. Sam had fallen asleep on her couch, intentionally this time.

Sam swung his legs off the couch and patted the cushions, searching for the phone that wouldn't stop ringing. *It's probably my father. Who else would keep calling over and over again?*

Ginger came out of the bedroom, wrapped in a flannel robe. "Are you going to answer that?"

Sam laughed. "Can't find it."

Ginger dropped to her knees and reached under the couch. "Aha. Here it is!" She triumphantly pulled the phone out and glanced at the screen. The smile left her face as she silently handed it to Sam.

He looked at the screen, and his stomach twisted as he answered. "Hey, Quinn," Sam said, shooting Ginger a look of apology.

"Hey, Sam." Quinn's voice sounded soft and familiar. "I'll be home on Wednesday, but I wanted to talk to you before then."

I can't talk to her while I'm here. "I'm kind of in the middle of something. Can I call you in half an hour?"

"Yeah. Is it something with your dad?"

"What?"

"You sound frazzled. Like you do when there's an issue with Trent."

"Yeah, yeah, that's it." Sam needed to escape Ginger's gaze.

He bid Quinn goodbye and ended the call then pulled on his jeans and his shirt. He grabbed his jacket and jammed his cell into the pocket. Before he went out the door, he told Ginger, "I'll be in touch."

Thirty minutes later, sprawled on his bed, Sam called Quinn.

"Hey, Sam," she said. "Is everything okay?"

"I'm surprised to hear from you."

"I've missed you. This break has shown me I don't want to be with anyone but you." Quinn's voice caressed him. "I'm truly sorry for the things I did, not answering your texts and being short on the phone."

A month ago, these words would have brought Sam joy, but now he was just confused. "I have to ask—were you with anyone?" He didn't want to hear her answer, but not knowing would kill him.

He heard Quinn take a deep breath. "No. There was one guy. It didn't take me long to figure out that he isn't half the man you are. Our love is special. I want to spend my life with you—no doubts. I love you, Sam."

Fuck, fuck, fuck. I feel so guilty for what I did with Ginger.

"Have you been with anyone?" she asked.

I can't tell her. "No." A long moment of silence stretched between them, then Sam asked, "When do you want to get together?"

"I won't be home until late on Wednesday, and my parents have something planned for Thanksgiving Day. Can you come over that night?"

"That will work. I love you, Quinn." *Shit.*

Sam drove back to Ginger's apartment later that afternoon. She answered the door in the same robe she'd been wearing that morning. "Can I come in?" he asked.

Ginger didn't say a word, just stepped back and waved her arm, indicating it was okay. She sat on the couch and picked up a glass of wine from the coffee table where the bottle, nearly empty, sat beside it.

The recliner was free of the laundry that had been piled there earlier, and Sam sank into it. "Quinn wants to end the break. She knows I'm the one she wants to be with." He gripped the arms of the chair. "I'm really sorry. I hope I didn't mislead you."

"I knew the score before we started." Ginger cocked her head. "Is this what you want?"

Sam rubbed his jaw. "I hadn't even looked at another woman in three years before you. You're very appealing, but I *love* Quinn. I owe it to her and to our relationship to see if those feelings are still there." He stood to leave.

"Sam, wait." Ginger rose and put her hand on his arm. "If the feelings aren't there, you know where to find me. It won't be easy to end things if that's what you decide to do. I can help you figure out what to say."

Chapter Eleven

Goodbye

Sam

On Thanksgiving afternoon, Sam desperately wanted to get away from his father. *Why is a holiday an excuse for him to drink even more than normal?*

He walked into the Whistle Stop, planning to play pool until he left to go to Quinn's house. The bar was almost empty, in stark contrast to its usual atmosphere. But he noticed Ginger sitting at a corner table.

I can't ignore her.

Sam and Quinn had talked often since Saturday, sometimes more than once a day. During the first few calls, thoughts of Ginger dueled with the reality of Quinn's soft, sexy words, but they faded as his feelings for Quinn were reawakened. Every morning, he awoke to a new text from Quinn, which caused the same rush of emotion he'd experienced when he was a senior in high school and just getting to know her. He felt like their relationship was back to where it had been when she'd left in August.

The night before Thanksgiving, Sam had dug under his clothes and retrieved the engagement ring. As he had twirled it in his fingers, his whole body felt alive. The proposal scenarios he'd concocted when the ring had initially arrived came back to him, playing over and over in his mind. He wondered if he should propose now, rather than waiting until Christmas as he'd told her he would.

Before he'd left for the Whistle Stop, Sam had slid the ring into his pocket. Now he reached in and touched the metal circle. His stomach twisted, and his cock hardened as he imagined Quinn's reaction. *I love her so much.*

Sam glanced over at Ginger. *It was the loneliness that drew me to her. I need to tell her that Quinn and I will be staying together, even though I know it's not what Ginger wants to hear.*

Even so, Sam's feet remained rooted to the floor, and he sipped a beer, pretending to watch a football game. Apprehension about how Ginger would react swirled over him. Remembering Ginger on her knees with her mouth on his cock made his stomach twist again. He shook his head, trying to dislodge the image.

I can't ever let Quinn find out how far things went with Ginger. It would crush her, even though we didn't technically...

A commotion at Ginger's table interrupted his thoughts.

Sam heard Ginger spit out, "You have to tell him!"

Sam turned to see who she was talking to. Her voice sounded more pissed than Sam had ever heard. *What the hell?*

Julie and Casey were standing by Ginger's table, and Julie's eyes were shooting firebolts at Ginger. "Mind your business!" Julie told her. "Just stay out of it!"

Sam slid off his barstool and walked over to the table. "What's going on?"

"Julie has something she needs to tell you." Ginger looked pointedly at Quinn's best friend.

"*No,* I don't," Julie said. "Ginger thinks she heard something, but it's not her concern."

Sam's breath caught. "What did you hear, Ginger?"

Ginger hesitated. "It's about what Quinn did in Virginia. Tell him, Julie."

"It's not my story to tell." Tears appeared in Julie's eyes. "I promised Quinn. It's not important, Sam. She loves you."

"You tell him, or I will," Ginger shot back before taking Sam's hand in hers. "He deserves to know."

"She... she... She slept with someone." Julie stammered it softly through tears.

Sam staggered as if someone had shoved him. "What did you say?"

Quinn slept with someone. Julie can't have said that. I must have heard it wrong.

Julie stood silently, one hand over her mouth and the other grasping Casey's arm.

Ginger was still holding Sam's hand, and he shook free of her. When Julie didn't answer, Sam said, more forcefully this time, "I asked you to repeat what you said."

Julie's continued refusal to answer told Sam what he needed to know. As he stood frozen in shock, Ginger reached to embrace him.

"Get away from me," he barked. He took a step back and continued to glare at Julie. "When?"

Julie's hand moved away from her mouth, and she said something Sam couldn't hear.

"*When* did she sl...sl...sl..." The word stuck in Sam's throat. "When?" he begged as tears began to fill his eyes.

"A couple of weekends ago," Julie replied softly.

She lied. Visions from the last three years flashed through Sam's mind. The day she fell into his arms as a shy fifteen-year-old, their first date almost a year later, the first time they'd made love, the way he'd held her as she cried before leaving in August, that night in the bell tower. They had always promised to be honest with each other.

All the phone calls and text messages since Saturday. She told me how much she loved me and missed me. I asked if she was with anyone, and she said she wasn't.

Is it all lies?

Ginger reached out to him again. "You'll be okay. It's better to know."

Sam turned to leave but heard Julie's voice echoing in the nearly empty bar as he walked away.

"Sam, it's not important," Julie pleaded. "It showed her where her heart is. She wants *you*."

Quinn

Quinn's nerve endings tingled in anticipation of seeing Sam. As soon as his headlights turned into her driveway on Thursday evening, she opened the door, bouncing on the balls of her feet. Sam walked toward her but slowly, and unable to hold back, she jumped down the two steps to the patio and ran over to throw her arms around him, laughing.

"I thought you'd never get here! Hey, hug me," she admonished him as his arms remained at his sides.

Then she realized Sam was breathing heavily, just before he said, "Let's go inside."

Quinn's bright smile dimmed when she pulled back and saw Sam's face. "What's the matter?"

"Did you sleep with someone in Virginia?"

Why is he asking me this again? Her body heated, and she felt the blush spreading over her cheeks. They hadn't moved from the driveway, and Quinn was grateful for the darkness. *I've never lied to him.* Dylan's first gentle kiss as they sat on the wall flashed through her mind. *Should I tell Sam about that? Will it be enough to admit to the kiss?*

She looked at Sam. His face was twisted with anger she'd only seen on him once before, after he'd had a confrontation with his father.

Sam's eyes bored into Quinn's. "Answer me!"

"No!"

"Tell me the truth, dammit." His voice shook.

I can't tell him any of it. "No, I wouldn't do that." Her eyes filled with tears. *I've never seen him like this.*

"Why are you crying?" Anger replaced the shakiness in Sam's voice.

His anger shocked her. Quinn knew Sam worked hard to control his temper because he didn't want to be like his father. "Because... because you're angry, and I feel like you're accusing me. You said we could do whatever we wanted to while we were on the break. And now—now, I don't know what you want." She took a step back. "You're scaring me. Why are you acting like this?"

Sam took a deep breath. "You think I'm accusing you? Did you do something to be accused of? I just want to know what you did." His voice was cold.

Quinn gave him a hard stare. "What did *you* do?"

Sam's face crumpled. "I... Nothing."

"What about the girl? The one that both Sylvie and Julie told me was after you? You slept at her apartment!"

"We didn't... I didn't have sex with her."

Quinn's tears slowed, replaced by a growing anger that matched Sam's. "Because the great Sam Carpenter has that much self-control? A pretty girl threw herself at you, and you did nothing? I don't believe you."

"You had sex, and you're lying about it."

How stupid have I been? First, I agree with Sam that we should take a break, then I get involved with Dylan, not realizing that all he wanted was to get in my pants.

Rage bubbled up inside Quinn. Rage at Dylan for misleading her and at Sam for his accusing questions. *And dammit... I'm mad at myself.* She looked at the ground, trying to control herself. She needed to figure out how to salvage things with Sam.

Working to keep the anger out of her voice, she said, "You told me I could spend my time however I wanted. I didn't know there'd be an inquisition at the end."

"I didn't know you'd spend your time whoring around."

Whack! Without thinking, Quinn slapped Sam's cheek. "How dare you?" She started to tremble and struggled to draw air into her lungs. *I've never hit anyone before. But calling me a whore? How could he?*

Sam reeled backward from the impact of her hand, his cheek red. "I can't be here." He walked away from her. "Do whatever you want, Quinn. We're over." He yanked open the car door, climbed inside and pulled it shut with a *bang* that reverberated through the quiet November night.

"Sam, no!" Quinn cried. "Come back!" Her legs felt like wood—she couldn't move from her spot on the drive, but her gaze was trained on Sam as he started the car. He sat for a moment, and Quinn could see the pain contorting his expression.

Their eyes met, tears streaming down both their faces.

"I'll tell you everything," she called. "Please, Sam, don't leave me."

His car door opened briefly, and Quinn took a step toward him. But then the door slammed again, and Sam shook his head, mouthing the word "no," before he backed up his car and drove out of her life.

Present Day

Quinn Michaels's head snapped up as footsteps sounded behind her in the darkened auditorium. She was sitting on the aisle at a conference titled Healthy Living in the Workplace, and the lecture hall was packed for introductions and the keynote address. Her early arrival had been timed to give her a choice of where to sit, and relief surged over her when the lights dimmed, and the adjacent seat was still empty. The footsteps drew closer.

The loser who just walked in forty-five minutes late is going to want that empty spot. She had placed her tote bag on the vacant seat, hoping to keep it for herself. *I hate how I still try to isolate myself in crowds.*

Quinn felt the tap on her shoulder. "Dammit." She moved her tote bag and swung her legs into the aisle, turning her head as the latecomer squeezed by. *What kind of person walks into a conference nearly an hour late?*

The man now seated next to her was breathing like he'd run a marathon. Quinn sighed. She was still aggravated, but that didn't overshadow her sympathy for the guy. She suspected the weekday Boston traffic probably did him in.

Turning her head slightly to look at the latecomer, she found him with his elbows on his knees and his head in his hands. He seemed wiry, but Quinn could see the outline of his bicep through his gray shirt. His brown hair was short, and his hands caught her attention. Her stomach jumped with the realization that he looked a lot like Sam Carpenter, her high school boyfriend. She couldn't see his face, but the hair, his build, the angle of his neck, and those hands all reminded her of Sam. Her head whipped back around. *No! There's no way Sam would be at a conference like this.*

She tried to look again without being obvious, but his face was still buried in his hands.

Her heart pounded wildly, and the heat of panic flooded her body. *I've got to get out of here!*

Acknowledgements

Heartfelt thanks to Mary Morris at Red Adept Editing for helping me to bring this story to fruition. Also to Sally Walker and Sheryl Soffer for telling me what worked and what didn't. Emily Hensley has been an inspiration, and I look forward to a long partnership.

My husband Gordy is always first in my heart for his patience and support.

And of course, you the readers. I appreciated the time you take to read my work and hope you enjoy reading it as much as I enjoy writing it.

About the author

Sue is an avid reader who ventured into the writing world during the first year of the Pandemic. Her stories showcase men and women working to become whole and happy. Family plays a prominent role as do the steamy encounters which come with falling in love.

Sue is a lifelong Vermonter who counts books, sunsets, and travel as vital to her being. Mountains, from the slopes of Vermont's Green Mountains to the towering peaks of Colorado's Rockies feed her soul.

Her children are grown and flown and she's living her happily ever after with the boy she met in a college library almost fifty years ago.

Follow her on Facebook at Sue Mills-Author.

Visit her website to stay up to date on new book releases. suemillsauthor.com